THE SPIRITS OF THE EARTH

THE SWISS LIST

CATHERINE COLOMB

THE SPIRITS OF THE EARTH

TRANSLATED BY JOHN TAYLOR

LONDON NEW YORK CALCUTTA

swiss arts council

prohelvetia

This publication has been supported by a grant from
Pro Helvetia, Swiss Arts Council

Seagull Books, 2016

Catherine Colomb, *Les Esprits de la terre* © CRLR (UNIL), Lausanne
English translation and Introduction © John Taylor, 2016

ISBN 978 0 85742 372 6

Typeset by Seagull Books, Calcutta, India
Printed and bound by Maple Press, York, Pennsylvania, USA

CONTENTS

In her native Switzerland, Catherine Colomb (1892–1965) has long been considered one of the most unusual and inventive francophone novelists of the twentieth century. Born into a well-off family of vintners who had settled in Saint-Prex on the shore of Lake Geneva, Marie-Louis Colomb—her real name—was an early orphan: her mother died when she was five. She was thereafter raised by her grandmother who eventually took her to Lausanne to attend school. She studied literature at the University of Lausanne, attaining the doctoral level and almost finishing her thesis on the Swiss travel writer Béat-Louis de Muralt (1665–1749). After her marriage in 1921 to Jean Reymond, a solicitor, Colomb devoted most of her time to her family, raising their two sons but at the same time secretly beginning to write. Using the penname Catherine Tissot, she published her first novel *Pile ou Face* (Heads or Tails) in 1934. Her second novel, *Châteaux en enfance* (Castles in Childhood, 1945), originally entitled *Les Chemins de Mémoire* (The Paths of Memory), drew attention to her work. Using her maiden family name (but not her true first name), Colomb entered the manuscript in a competition whose jury consisted of the well-known publisher H. L. Mermod as well as five important Swiss writers and critics: Paul Budry, Edmond Jaloux, Gustave Roud, C. F. Ramuz and Albert Mermoud. The jury did not award her the prize but gave special mention to the manuscript's 'remarkable quality', all the while noting that its unconventionality was not entirely suitable for the contest rules. Colomb's next novel, *Les Esprits de la terre* (The Spirits of the Earth, 1953), was a critical success. The author was widely recognized as an exceptional new voice and this reputation was confirmed when a fourth novel, *Le Temps des anges* (The Time of Angels or Angel Time), appeared in 1962. When she died three years later, Colomb had not quite finished a new novel, *Les Royaumes combattants* (The Fighting Realms), and a long story, *La Valise* (The Suitcase).

Except for stays, when she was a teenager and a young woman, in Weimar, Potsdam, Berlin, Paris and London (where she met members of the Bloomsbury Circle, including Lloyd George, Bertrand Russell, Lytton Strachey and Vaslav Nijinksy—but not the Woolfs), Colomb spent her entire life in the canton of Vaud, living in Yverdon-les-Bains, Lausanne and Prilly. Her novels are inspired by her family origins and much informed by her sharp observations of the other affluent families of the area. She participated very little in the Swiss literary life of the period. It is known that she read Honoré de Balzac, Friedrich Hölderlin, Jean Paul and especially Marcel Proust, as well as, late in life, Virginia Woolf; but, above all, she fashioned her exceptional style and formally innovative fiction in relative isolation.

The Spirits of the Earth is the first English translation of the second of the three novels that have established Colomb's lasting reputation. Like the two others, it is a family drama that takes place among settings that the author knew intimately—in the canton of Vaud. The story revolves around two (fictional) family properties, a château called Fraidaigue and a country mansion, the Maison d'En Haut. The château stands along the shore of Lake Geneva, whereas the mansion, as its name specifies, can be found in the hills higher up above the lake. It is not without pertinence to the novel that the prehistoric site 'Fraidaigue' (literally 'Cold Water'), near Saint-Prex, first consisted of two Neolithic lakeshore villages before being taken over by the Gallic Helvetii tribe and then by the Romans. In *The Spirits of the Earth*, Colomb alludes several times to 'ancient' periods.

The intricately composed central character, César, is the eldest child of a family that consists of one sister,

Zoé, and two other brothers, Eugène and Adolphe. César has not claimed, and, in fact, has by no means been encouraged to claim, his rightful share to a part of the heritage (and thus to at least one of the properties) that has been left to the children after the deaths of their parents. The mother's death has especially been devastating for César. She is called 'la tourterelle' or, in English, 'the turtledove' in the novel; unlike a nickname, the word bears a conspicuous small *t*. Moreover, the proximity between 'colomb' (dove) and turtledove is obvious, a connection that is all the more poignant in that the author lost her own mother at a young age. The reader learns later on in the plot that the father's death has occurred shortly after his wife's fall from the château roof, where she had been trying to pick a clump of maidenhair fern.

César is thus a 'nomad' or, to use the English acronym that Colomb herself employs in her French prose, a 'D.P.' (displaced person). He lives for six months of the year in the lakeshore château, now taken over by his younger brother Eugène and his intimidating wife (austerely called 'Madame' and nicknamed 'Semiramis'). At every autumnal equinox, he moves from this château up to the country mansion claimed by Adolphe after his marriage to Mélanie, the daughter of a man of modest origins who has made lots of money. César then stays at 'their' house for six months. As in Balzac's novels, 'old' and 'new' money, not to mention interfamilial scheming, create the socioeconomic antagonisms brought forth with such acuity and mordant humour in *The Spirits of the Earth*.

César is a sometimes pitiless, sometimes pitiful, ever fascinating character for whom the reader entertains an uncomfortable sympathy from the onset. In the opening scene, he has probably removed a stone from the château cornice so that his nephew Abraham, whom he has encouraged to edge his way along it, will fall to his death. And yet various passages also underscore César's love for Abraham and his other nephew, Ulysse, who is handicapped because of an act that will startle the reader when it is recounted much later in the narrative. Abraham and Ulysse, both of whom are Eugène and Madame's children, also have a sister, Isabelle. Isabelle has still not received a marriage proposal, often because Madame, who has a penchant for staring, chases potential suitors off. The pathetically well-meaning Isabelle keeps repeating that such and such a suitor had been in love with her and had intended to marry her, but that it was she 'who didn't want to'.

As for César, he views his adulthood as a brutal separation from a sort of paradise. He mostly lives in a dream world made up of his lost childhood and his vanished playmates. He intends to find them once again, suspecting that he will come across them one day in his favourite haunt: a marshy beach-like area, near the château. There he spends much of his time lying on his back and ruminating. Strangely, these vanished figures from his childhood also include his two brothers and sister, as an early passage specifies. Who, then, in this novel, is alive and who is dead? Is everyone dead? 'Where are my brothers, my sister from back then? Where are the children?' César notably asks, not long after the dramatic opening scene: 'In my dreams, I meet up with them, they're standing on the beach, I speak to them, I touch their chubby little hands. [. . .] Yet they're not dead, one would have known so if they were.'

This is why the opening scene, which initially seems to entail either an accident or a murder, increasingly takes on strangeness and ambiguity as the plot unfolds on several levels of time and consciousness. Has Abraham really died? Has he possibly come back to life, as later scenes show? Has César's childhood truly vanished for ever? Are the missing children and siblings whom he constantly searches for perhaps actually hiding out somewhere in the environs? Or, once again, are they all dead? And where, ultimately, is César? On the earth? In the earth?

These and similar questions arise in a narrative that initially and then increasingly seems based on a multilayered indeterminacy. The double setting of the château and the country mansion, the plot combining elements of both ghost stories and sardonic family chronicles, and the handful of rich parvenus and impoverished upper-class characters whose faltering income depends on favourable wine harvests that never occur enable Colomb to build a psychologically penetrating and formally bold story in which the living and the dead intermingle and in which Time is itself a central mystery.

What, indeed, is Time in this troubling novel? A sort of 'time of angels' or 'angel time', as the title of Colomb's novel *Le Temps des anges* suggests? In other words, Time as viewed or experienced by angels and not by human beings in their flesh and blood? Are the characters in fact 'angels' of sorts, present on the earth in these particular settings—the château and the Maison d'En Haut—with their respective histories full of tragic, comic and tragicomic events? Or are the characters and all the events ultimately perceived or recollected by one character, César, who thus has a somehow 'angelic' vantage point? An underground angelic perspective, it must be specified, if the stunningly beautiful last scene in the novel is taken into account.

The reader will ponder such questions. Colomb shifts between placing herself fully in a character's mind—there are various distinct narrative 'I's'—and speaking as an omniscient narrator in a disturbing 'here and now', which, in fact, encompasses or superposes the past, the present and the future. It is often as if the novelist blends or inverts segments of the past, the present and the future on the time line. This narrative 'here and now' is thus remarkably dense because 'here' is not just here and 'now' is not merely now: they are multidimensional. Moreover, as she creates Boléro-like effects through intentional repetitions and leitmotifs (the maidenhair fern, the château tower demolished by the father after the turtledove's death, a particular bend in the road leading to the Maison d'En Haut, the ancient vases that fishermen drag up in their nets, a fiacre progressing through the haze, lightweight pebbles left on a windowsill, cleaning one's fingernails, embroidery work, the liquid manure in the old pigsty), Colomb allows key scenes to recur yet depicts them from slightly different angles; factual descriptions yield to dialogues, to indirect discourse, or to stream-of-consciousness; and throughout, the author focuses on disquieting details with her microscope. Even as the château walls are 'tilted', the entire story seems positioned at an odd angle to the cosmos.

These modernist and, as some commentators have pointed out, New Novel narrative techniques that Colomb forged all by herself—she never read any of the French New Novelists—are amply visible in her three major novels. As the poet José-Flore Tappy, who is also the general editor of Colomb's collected works at L'Âge d'Homme (the edition that I have used for this translation), has observed in regard to the unfinished novel *Les Royaumes combattants*, the novelist 'touches upon the gravest subjects under the guise of volubility. Conversations, episodes, and fanciful digressions form the mesh of a large net that she tries to toss over a prey that remains ever remote and ungraspable.'[1]

Colomb was fascinated by the processes of memory and consciousness. It is not surprising that her work has been compared to Woolf's novels and Proust's *À la recherche du temps perdu*. One could add Henry James because of her ironic depictions of the suave meanness governing family relationships. Balzac as well, as has been mentioned in regard to Colomb's scrutiny of socioeconomic pressures, especially when they create a victim such as César (who is, at the same time, his own victim). The novelist's bizarre combination of social satire and the supernatural also brings Jean Paul to mind. This is not to forget that her sarcastic portrayals of some characters' behaviour or ways of speaking are very funny. Colomb's depiction of how Zoé goes mad, or feigns to go mad, prefigures the analyses of anti-psychiatry.

Although such literary affinities can be spotted, they are, ultimately, just that: affinities. Colomb has a singular tone and a unique way of constructing a novel, a manner all her own of staging time, of depicting events and of exploring the workings of memory and consciousness. Many outstanding Swiss writers and poets, including José-Flore Tappy, Anne Perrier, Jacques Chessex, Gustave Roud and Philippe Jaccottet, have devoted essays to her work and acknowledged their admiration. In Roud's preface to a 1968 edition of Colomb's three novels, the prose poet declares: 'Anyone who crosses the threshold of these books feels marvellously astray.'[2] For Roud, this initial sentiment of bewilderment is a necessary passage enabling the reader to approach Colomb's singular use of memory and narrative time. In the same essay, Roud defines her *oeuvre* as a 'unique place for reunion, where the double mystery of space and time is effaced and the border between the realm of the living and that of the dead is abolished.'[3] Another supporter was the ever-perspicuous Jean Paulhan, who published *Le Temps des anges* at Gallimard in 1962. In a letter dated 2 August 1951, he wrote to Gaston Gallimard: 'I think that I have found a novelist who is a genius.'[4]

Rather like Roud, Jaccottet, reviewing *Les Esprits de la Terre* for the *Nouvelle Revue de Lausanne* as early as 1953, notes:

> [T]he reader who ventures into this novel finds himself in somewhat the same situation as a man whom chance, a false address, or an unexpected storm has suddenly ushered amidst a family who nonetheless keeps on living without paying any attention to him. [. . .] The novel begins with no introduction, no explanation, no exposition (as one says in the theatre). Instead, there are a thousand allusions to events or characters that are still unknown to us, as happens in family jargons that are comprehensible only to members of the tribe. Such a style may discourage readers who are in a hurry; but a good writer never works for such readers.[5]

Colomb certainly seeks to record, as faithfully as possible, the workings of minds permeated with recollected scenes and conversations, musings, even hallucinations, not to mention the issue of whether these 'minds' dwell in the realm of the living or in that of the dead, or if these 'minds' are in fact incarnated in a single mind—César's—that has absorbed them, as it were. Colomb's novelistic solutions to these multifarious challenges are initially unsettling: one has the impression of entering a maze, an image in fact evoked in *The Sprits of the Earth* when Hampton Court is mentioned with respect to an English governess who gets lost in it. But as Jaccottet suggests, Colomb's method increasingly convinces. One gets used to it. And actually quite quickly, one finds oneself drawn ever-more deeply into a novel that is by no means without suspense.

'Does life go on according to an outline?' wrote Colomb of her own books in 1964, one year before she died:

> Doesn't memory constantly intervene, creating a parallel life, bringing along hundreds of recollections, fleeting visions, and daydreams until, suddenly—you don't know why—everything vanishes and for an instant subsists only the image of periwinkle growing around a grave or, in a parlour, white rose petals slowly dropping off and plunking down on the beige felt tablecloth embroidered with gold thread? […] My three novels could be called *The Paths of Memory*. […] It's a countless crowd, made up of the dead and the living, who leaves the age-old nooks and fragments of time and teem over the paths of memory. Space is where the living are; time is the realm of the dead.[6]

Translating Colomb's prose is no easy chore. English equivalents must be found for prose that leaps between factual description, direct discourse, indirect discourse and stream-of-consciousness, not to mention the novelist's unusual use of verbal tenses (and thus visions of the past and present). Her frequent use of the imperfect tense is especially conspicuous. Sometimes she translates an action frequently repeated in the past; in such cases, English solutions such as 'she would go' or 'she often came', etc., are appropriate. But at other times it is as if Colomb were reliving or reimagining a scene (in the imperfect tense) before writing it down; she wants to see the act happening again, in all its continuity and duration, and chooses to record it, not as an accomplished act in the simple past (as in the English preterit 'she went', etc.) but, rather, in that very state of *happening again*: 'she was going'. In the same way, she also often juxtaposes two independent acts occurring simultaneously. An early example:

> César was sneaking away from the haze-covered lake while a fisherman was rowing out from behind the headland and, with a stroke of his oar, already drifting over the deep water.

A little further on, Colomb uses four verbs in the imperfect tense in a sentence that also employs direct discourse:

'In the past,' Madame was explaining to the next suitor, Benjamin, who was making his first stay as a student missionary and who was clasping under his arm a book which related conversions of Africans and which he was hoping to pawn off on them for the long winter evenings, 'we organized children's balls with paper lanterns for Isabelle, Abraham and Ulysse. Poor Ulysse!'

In these and many other cases, Colomb wants to recover, before the act of writing, the sensation of continuity and simultaneity.

These stylistic idiosyncrasies, with their philosophical implications (once again, the notion of 'angelic time' is appropriate), are compounded by Colomb's punctuation, which Tappy qualifies, in her edition, as 'often much more emotional or rhythmic than grammatical'. Colomb uses quotation marks to set off utterances in direct discourse, as many writers do, but there are also instances where she does not use quotation marks for utterances that nonetheless seem to be examples of direct discourse or, at least, of fully articulated thoughts in the mind of a character. I have respected her choices in these cases, using quotation marks where she has done so and not using them where she has not. Different levels of narrative, that is, of the narrator's or the character's consciousness, are involved. In the following example, one would have expected quotation marks setting off 'Order had been restored . . . will kill me' and 'I who have such frail health . . . out of sheer willpower', but there are no quotation marks in the original:

> Order had been restored, but these alerts will
> kill me, Madame was saying, I who have such
> frail health and remain on my feet only out of
> sheer willpower.

Such cases, furthermore, raise the question of who is narrating.

Another translation quandary arises with colons, semicolons, commas and full stops. Even as Colomb uses two or more verbs of the imperfect tense to show two acts taking place simultaneously in the past, she also sometimes takes two or three complete assertions, which each could have ended with a full stop, and, separating them with a comma, aligns them into a single long sentence. Once again, with a few exceptions (where I have inserted a semicolon instead of a comma to avoid semantic ambiguities in English), I have mirrored her punctuation since she is clearly experimenting, in such case, with the possibilities of expressing unexpected connections and continuities.

Finally, there is some English used in the French original. With a couple of exceptions (where Colomb italicizes a French word in her text as well), all the words or phrases in italics, in this translation, are also in English in the original.

Let me express my gratitude to five Swiss friends who were instrumental in helping me to translate this novel. It was the translator and literary-magazine editor Marion Graf who first introduced me to the work of Catherine Colomb, kindly putting a copy of *Châteaux en enfance* into my hands one day, in November 2010, at the Looren Translation House, and telling me that I would surely like the novel. She was right! José-Flore Tappy, whose work I also translate, was encouraging from the onset, answering my questions and sympathizing with my doubts, as was the critic Doris Jakubec, ever willing to share her knowledge of the writings of Colomb and of countless other Swiss authors. The scholar Daniel Maggetti, who is an expert on Colomb's vocabulary, helpfully clarified troublesome words, with obsolete meanings, notably where transportation is involved. When Colomb writes *voiture*, she does not necessarily mean 'automobile' ... And my heartfelt thanks go to Félicie Girardin, who is Catherine Colomb's granddaughter, and to the other descendants of the novelist, for giving me permission to translate this remarkable *oeuvre*. I would also like to acknowledge the Centre de Recherches sur les Lettres

Romandes at the University of Lausanne and the Sonia Raiziss Charitable Foundation, which awarded me a grant enabling me to see this translation through to the end.

John Taylor

Notes

1 Catherine Colomb, *Œuvres complètes*, VOL. 3 (*La Valise / Les Royaumes combattants*) (Lausanne: L'Âge d'Homme, 1993), p. 14.

2 Gustave Roud, preface to Catherine Colomb, *Œuvres* (Lausanne: L'Aire / Rencontre, 1968), pp. 7–25. Reprinted in Catherine Colomb, *Œuvres complètes*, VOL. 1 (*Châteaux en enfance / Les Esprits de la Terre*) (Lausanne: L'Âge d'Homme, 1993), p. 13.

3 Ibid., p. 25.

4 Jean Paulhan and Gaston Gallimard, *Correspondance 1919–1968* (Laurence Bisset ed.) (Paris: Gallimard, 2011). Paulhan had actually received the manuscript of *Les Esprits de la Terre* when he made this remark to Gallimard. But the manuscript was eventually rejected by the publisher. In his first letter (dated 26 July 1947) to Gallimard about Colomb, Paulhan wrote: 'A year ago, a rather surprising book appeared at the Guilde du Livre and it went unnoticed: Catherine Colomb's *Châteaux d'enfance*. I think that I will suggest that you accept it for the NRF.' Only Colomb's third novel, *Le Temps des anges*, would be published (in 1962) by Gallimard.

5 Philippe Jaccottet, *Nouvelle Revue de Lausanne*, 23 April 1953. Reprinted in *Écrits pour papier journal: Chroniques, 1951–1970* (Paris: Gallimard, 1994), p. 49.

6 Catherine Colomb, *Gazette littéraire* (Lausanne), 7–8 December 1968. Reprinted in *Œuvres complètes*, VOL. 2 (*Le Temps des anges / Pile ou face*) (Lausanne: L'Âge d'Homme, 1993), p. 7.

THE SPIRITS OF THE EARTH

'Abraham has just fallen!'

'From the tower?'

'No, not from the tower, from the cornice!'

'But, my God, what was he doing on the cornice?'

'It's César who pushed him!'

'César!'

'César!'

'Fancy that,' mused the messenger as she heard the shouting, 'I'd have thought it was Monsieur César who'd been killed by Madame.'

In the hallways of Fraidaigue, one will henceforth have to meet up with dead Abraham attending to his transparent affairs while running into his mother whose head is topped off with some snowy construction, his sister Isabelle surrounded by her suitors, and his deformed little brother Ulysse pressing a black marble inkpot against his chest with his dwarfed arm. And Uncle César? Where's Uncle César? His dear nephew has just fallen from the cornice, and he has vanished? This is because he leaves, like every autumn, for the Maison d'En Haut, walking along the wall of Fraidaigue, diverting his eyes because of a clump of maidenhair fern, while the little manservant of the Maison d'En Haut is already raising his hand to protect himself from César's blows and the little manservant of Fraidaigue, leaning against the doorframe, is at last breathing the pure air of an evening of reprieve. The women servants are sweeping the room where César stays for six months every year, nothing remains in there any more except a green rep half-curtain, the other half having been stolen by the messenger that night when Armand was finishing off the demolition of the half-ruined tower from which the turtledove had fallen while picking some maidenhair fern and when he had spotted the diligent messenger taking away the dead child's long embroidered dresses in her wicker cart. Frightened, César and his little brothers were sitting on their beds and listening to stones thudding down on the white roses which, the night before, were hesitating at the edge of the young coffin. 'Tell us, César, are those dull sounds we're hearing, waves?' César shook his head, he had freckles and thick red hair. Now those carrot-red hairs were sewn one by one onto a felt disk and he was leaving furtively, like every autumn, for the Maison d'En Haut. Rim, the penniless cousin who was living with his wife, out of Madame's charity, in the former pigsty ('You'll be fine there,' she

4

had said, 'so much freer than in the château. And, of course, you don't need to come to the parlour when I have visitors. Stay in the peace and quiet of your pretty little house. I'm the one who'd rather be there instead of at this enormous Fraidaigue . . . '), was stepping right over the mud wallow and was delighted to be holding up wounded Abraham from behind as he was being carried up the staircase; drops of blood were staining the worn steps that are so soft to the feet of dead women coming down during their first night to fetch a glass of water. Abraham had fallen all the way down to the narrow beach, Uncle César had vanished, Madame was accusing him: 'It's César!'

'But darling,' Eugène was timidly protesting, 'César . . . '

'Where's your brother right now, do you happen to know? And how does he spend all that time in the stable? When he leaves, he's tipsy. He drinks, I tell you. So go to the stable! Go see him, talk to him; it's not up to me, it's not my family . . . Oh! If only I had known!'

When the fiacre was taking her to the ball in the fog and an old man, walking along the snow-covered pavement, gave her his hand.

'Oh! That César is my cross, he's . . . '

'But darling, if he asked for his share?'

'His share! He ate it up ages ago; he's been eating at our table and sleeping in my sheets for twenty-five years now. And, if I may ask: How can we get Isabelle married with that individual in the family? Think of that French officer—she already imagined . . . She would embroider lace from morning to night because he would say, "Oh, Mademoiselle Isabelle, don't you do needle lace? All the young girls at home . . . " Why did that officer sneak off without letting us know? And Benjamin? She would read every book published on the Basel Mission. And Julien? Oh! Oh! César, my cross!'

She began groaning so loudly that the startled villagers stuck their heads out of their windows: 'It's the baroness. What's the matter with her? Let's hope our windowpanes won't fall out as they did the other day!' The stranger tasting freshly pressed grape must on the inn terrace was surprised that the villagers didn't seem to hear the waves thudding against the rocks and spurting up against the walls of Fraidaigue; on the cornice running beneath the first-floor windows, a stone had been missing that evening.

'Be patient, darling,' ventured good-willed Eugène, 'be patient, the grapes are harvested, he's getting ready to leave.'

'That César, he's my cross. The sword of Damocles. Ah! Ah! It's all one and the same to me, after all. Let him claim his share, let him get married again, marry the shooting-gallery woman, the curator's niece, the engineer's daughter, the inn servant, or the one he chases after when he rides away on his bicycle on summer evenings and comes back home at dawn. Comes back from where? Do you happen to know? Of course you don't. Monsieur doesn't look after his brother. Monsieur loiters on the beach, helping fishermen pull in their nets, getting heaped with praise by the wine-growers because he gives them two litres instead of one at harvest time, and in the meantime César . . . '

And yet how he lives in clover! Six months here, six months there, with Adolphe and Mélanie. Put up, fed, furnished with light and clean laundry. His share? Just let him claim it!

She was vigorously cleaning the nails of her left hand with the ring finger of her right hand.

'But my God,' she suddenly cried out—the messenger and Ol' Miss Gibaude, both worried, leant out of their windows—'what if he did claim his share? Would we have to take out a mortgage on the château? With these bad wine years, what's left to pay the interest with?'

'No,' she quickly added in a hush: 'I see. He'll move in here with one of those girls. And we'll go to live in the stable instead of those poor Rims. (Has that egoist even once thought of those *poor* Rims?) Or else we'll hit the road with unwed Isabelle and Ulysse, poor Ulysse!, along with Abraham and his eternal flute.'

'But darling, we haven't reached that point yet.'

'Then what point have we reached, if I may ask?'

She stood up heavily, lividly white because she had been walled up for so long, her strong hands hanging straight down at her sides.

'Don't torment yourself, darling, the grapes are harvested, he's getting ready to leave.'

Indeed, César was sneaking away from the haze-covered lake while a fisherman was rowing out from behind the headland and, with a stroke of his oar, already drifting over the deep water. César the nomad, the D.P., sat down to catch his breath on his small rope-bound servant's suitcase, at that bend where you can see the fiery-coloured lake for the last time; the blue, pink or green pebbles which, as they are rolled around by the waves, lose their weight little by little and evolve into flowers of the waters, had faded with the coming of autumn. 'Where are my brothers, my sister from back then? Where are the children? In my dreams, I meet up with them, they're standing on the beach, I speak to them, I touch their chubby little hands. Between them and us, Zoé pretending to be crazy in order to escape pity, Adolphe with his weary wrinkled eyes behind his lorgnon, Eugène whose big rosy face sports the stripe of a salt-and-pepper moustache, and me...César...there's no resemblance, no possible comparison. Yet they're not dead, one would have known so if they were. They're living somewhere, waiting for me. Not at the Maison d'En Haut, in any case, on those grounds overgrown with high grass, trees, rye and potatoes, but, instead, right there on the bare earth of the beach, on the bare earth of the vineyards. To escape one day from Madame's watchfulness, wander with the children met, once again, inside the silent earth, come across yellow violets, vinestocks turned into iron!' César stood up, the embankment would hide the lake from sight for six months. Mélanie, who was on the lookout for him in the sycamore-lined avenue, raised her hand to her tumultuous breasts.

'Oh, César, what's happened? You're of course not the one who made Abraham fall? On the telephone, I said it wasn't true, since you'd arrived here yesterday evening. They won't find anything out. For all they care about you down there ...'

He walked by her without replying. In the garden, his sister Zoé was eating food that had been brought to her in a newspaper; she could stand neither the number 3 nor the word *if*. Wiping his lorgnon on the tip of his waistcoat, Adolphe emerged on the threshold.

'But César, you're here?'

'Since yesterday evening,' Mélanie said swiftly, 'he went to the woods early this morning, that's why you didn't see him.'

Now that's a useless lie. Poor Mélanie, ever ready to die for César. Abraham was so light that he suffered only a few scratches when he fell from the cornice; moreover, César had immediately regretted the removed stone. 'Come back, Abraham, come back!' he kept shouting at his nephew from the tower window. In his defence, it must be said that Madame, that evening, had acted like a Gorgon even more than usual: she kept scrutinizing César intently, just as stars do, focusing their stares on you during summer nights, so much so that frightened villagers clasp their hands and raise them to the sky; and then, without lifting her eyes from César, she alluded to mules, which cannot have offspring. Various signs indicated that she was going to burst out laughing and show her yellow deep-sea-diver teeth. A mule, indeed! This is why César the nomad, the D.P., tried to kill his nephew Abraham. Before the sun rose the next day, he ventured out on the cornice, the stone walkway which marked the limits of the world of children and against which their sky once leant. Glued to the wall, he moved cautiously in front of the fifteen windows. What if Madame awoke at that very moment! But no, she could be heard snoring. If they had listened well, they would have heard her snoring in the fiacre back then when an old man was walking alongside her in the fog. If she awoke, she would open the shutters, pushing César off into the void. No more return of the shepherd, the traveller, the hostile stranger, the fox without a hole, his carrot-red hair sewn one by one onto a felt disk! What a cross to see him coming back to Fraidaigue in mid March when the osier bushes are reddening around the streams and the bare earth of the vineyards is the colour of dawn! Suddenly, he would be pushed off and down to the rocks twenty feet below the windows. But Madame was sleeping, and César could edge his way along the narrow cornice; the wall was tilted somewhat because of ancient waves, and God knows what shells from the lake filled the room behind the painted window. The fishermen already far out on the lake and barely emerging from behind the headland were letting silent or adverse winds go by. Fraidaigue has only one tower left, but the demolished one can be heard shivering when the easterly Vaudaire wind blows, and the fishermen once again bring back ancient lake vases that they have dragged in with their nets. At the corner of the wall, a stone in the cornice was wobbly, César removed it, letting it fall noisily into the water. 'Come, Abraham,' he said a few hours later, 'you see, when we were small we'd follow the cornice all the way to the painted window.'

That a mason hanging between sky and water had sculpted with extreme care. Ah, if he had left it open so that the children could peek inside at the mahogany chest and the embroidery basket on the round table!

'Come, Abraham, you go ahead of me. Step over the window ledge.'

Abraham started out on the stone walkway, holding to his ear a grey lake shell all pearly inside and dreamily striated with brown.

'Come back, Abraham, come back,' César suddenly shouted.

If he had not been holding that shell, he would have been able to keep his balance at the corner of the tower, the spot where, that Wednesday evening, a stone was suddenly missing.

'Abraham has fallen!'

'From the tower?'

'No, not from the tower, from the cornice. It's César . . .'

Thinking he could now take over his dead brother's room, Ulysse carried his black marble inkpot to it. At the very moment when Abraham, resuscitated, swept Ulysse's inkpot away with his transparent arm, and the poor disappointed crippled boy had to go back to his bedroom enveloped in green shadow where he lived like a distorted tree, the man who would be Isabelle's last suitor—the man from the canton of Uri—arrived. On his skull was growing the magnifying glass of fifty-year-old men. Eleven brothers and sisters! Up by four o'clock to reap, each of them with five cows to milk before leaving for school, they don on Sundays starched shirts and garments made of fine black cloth, stroll with their old father who wears a gold earring, walks like a nutcracker and keeps a blue cotton umbrella and a sword tucked under his arm. The angelus tolls over the old land, a giants' stairway down which the Reuss River cascades. The mother prays aloud in the kitchen at the same time as the men in the fields and the valet in the stable; over the thick table with holes dug into it for soup, the little finger of her damp hand pushes away the letter of her married daughter in New York who goes out on the town only in automobiles and draped in a long grey-feathered boa. Nearly a hundred years old, the father has just come back inside. He calls out to the valet to unharness the four horses. Farm life is too hard! Of the eleven children, only Anna had stayed behind; the father had led them, one after another, his arm around their shoulders, to the limit of his fields, and then chased them off. 'I'm tired,' he said. He called Anna, tall and wide as a door, and asked for a glass of kirsch. 'Anna, my hour has come, I'm going to die.' She tossed an apron over her head and ran out to find the priest. A half-hour later, the father was dead. Régula came from Warsaw, the son from England rushed home, helped to carry the coffin, his braces mauve with designs in matching tones. They noticed, alongside, that dead boy from long ago, that thirteen-year-old child killed by the horses on the hill, now he was standing there, his little chest covered with dirt, his thick hands chapped with the first cold spells. It was therefore with a black band around his hat and with his thumbs in the armholes of his waistcoat that the man from the canton of Uri arrived at the château to deal with a sale of wine; he had a broad face, broader even than he himself imagined, and he was standing on the platform of a tramway in Zurich, eh? He punctuated his sentences with *eh*, constantly calling into doubt the existence of the dentist and his sister Naphtaly. Was it thus that I was standing on the platform, that my father was dead, and that my sister Naphtaly, smelling of camphor and pepper, was returning to Warsaw in the weighted-down train carriage in which Jews were being sent back, eh? He wanted to give his seat to a brown-clad woman who was wearing a purple veil and just leaving the dentist's. It was raining, the asphalt was again taking on its black colour from the centre of the globe (Earth! Earth!), the tramway abruptly jolted to the side, sliding on the wet rails and, eh, I was thrown to the ground and broke two ribs. The lady gave out a clove-scented scream. 'Would you like,' asked the busy doctor, his forehead periscope aiming to the right, to the left, at human misery, 'that is, could you stand having a bandage wrapped all around?' One morning at the clinic and that was it. Of course, sleeping with that rubber undershirt was impossible. But what would he have done for ten days in his bed now that there was a war and that he could henceforth buy only the wine from the lakeshore vineyards and sell it at a high price on the farthest border, in Appenzell? Nor had the Italian count been able to sleep in that same bedroom. No one ever saw the count; bread was brought to him, no one moved inside the flat, then the door would barely open, a hand would take the bread, the milk. He couldn't sleep, would gaze at his papers piled up along the walls and now and then absent-mindedly rummage through them, using his jade walking stick with its golden wrist loop, after which he would stand at the window, pushing aside the heavy Venetian curtain formerly held up by stucco angels and today by upholstery tacks and safety pins, and imagine he was seeing his persecutors straight across the lake, on the other shore, coming down from the mountains, groping to find at dawn the missing banister of a dilapidated stairway, now standing in boats still bearing the Cross of Savoy, and heading for him. He would sometimes read, full of hope, on the torn-off piece of newspaper in which his meat was wrapped, that one of those all-powerful Superior Beings who was playing with men as once did the gods, fairies and threatening Jesuits camped along the borders, had died of throat cancer in the depths of his château built in the clouds. Two twins reached the village, leant on the wall beneath the plane trees, stared at the count's windows. Sometimes they went down the streets lined with houses tilted because of ancient waves, returned without exchanging a word, leant on the wall and watched the count's windows. He remained sitting at his table, so motionless that emboldened sparrows would perch in the folds of his enormous white waistcoat and peck at the crumbs; he didn't dare to stand up, how could he make the twins believe it was only his valet, this face embellished with blond sideburns and topped with a boater, once known to all of Europe when he would ride up and down the French Riviera in his donkey-drawn buggy? He ventured raising a broom topped with a boater which was immediately shot right through by a bullet that also made a hole in portrait of the countess Clotilde, a painting that Isabelle had fortunately never seen, she could keep believing that it was she whom the count loved, that it was for her that he was hiding out on the first floor of the château-hotel and rocking back and forth in the red-velvet rocking chair he had inherited from the King of Naples. The twins kept on the lookout for the count for three days, the cigarette butts piled up on the wall where the maidenhair fern grows, the wall from which César would turn his eyes whenever he walked alongside it. The count finally came down, opened the door imitating that of a fortified castle, and surrendered. Studying the sky from the tower, Madame noticed the silent trio walking by. She was looking for the bird that sometimes came down from the mountains, gliding for a moment above the lake and then making big circles around the tower. 'How animals love me!' she would murmur. With her emphatic smile, Isabelle was daydreaming at her bedroom window and watching the count going away. He was wearing his boater. 'He'd have liked to marry me, he was always looking in this direction.' The man from the canton of Uri, who now occupied the count's room, couldn't sleep because of that damned bandage. But what would he have done, may I ask, if he had been confined for ten days in the clinic at harvest time?

'And at more than ninety years old, the father was still ploughing!' The man from the canton of Uri pulled out his jack-knife and cleaned his finger-nails. His sister, tall and wide as a door, whom the father, his arm around her shoulders, had led to the limits of the field, stepped back and forth in the boat, making it tip towards the water, and now she owned horses, automobiles, twelve silver-gilded little coffee spoons. Isabelle was listening to her tales and randomly sticking the pointless needle into the needle lace. 'Oh, Mademoiselle Isabelle, don't you do needle lace?' had asked with surprise the interned French officer with his little brown moustache and his beauty spot on his left cheek. At the bottom of his too-short blue tunic emerged a handsome pointed derrière. 'All the young girls in France . . . My mother . . .' This is why the man from the canton of Uri, as he entered the château, had to use his large hand to push away the needle lace hanging from the windows, from the doors, and around the lamps. Madame came in without a word and went out onto the balcony where she stood motionlessly; she was marching along against the backdrop of the waves at the same time as the earth was tilting towards the east. A draft of cold air was blowing in from her black-plush cape; she was lifting her broad face towards the sky where the faint glimmers of the equinox were still visible, Abraham was leaning out of the tower window, deformed Ulysse was wandering through the hallways, pressing a black-marble inkpot against his chest with his poor dwarfed arm. Madame finally turned around and the man from the canton of Uri, despite all his bravery, couldn't keep himself from wincing. Every movement pained him, eh? But could he remain in the clinic and miss the harvest? The wine-grower was dancing heavily on the beaten earth, with two dahlias stuck in his black leather cap, while the man from the canton of Uri was leaving the château, his wine sale clinched. Near the entrance pillars he turned around, Isabelle waved a goodbye and went back up to the parlour, murmuring, 'He'd have liked to marry me, I'm the one who didn't want him. When a man says, "Our house is heated by stoves, eh? Oh, how comfortable it is!", this means he'd like to have you.'

'In the past,' Madame was explaining to the next suitor, Benjamin, who was making his first stay as a student missionary and who was clasping under his arm a book which related conversions of Africans and which he was hoping to pawn off on them for the long winter evenings, 'we organized children's balls with paper lanterns for Isabelle, Abraham and Ulysse. Poor Ulysse!' Benjamin stood in awe of Madame who, happy to remember those lanterns, masked her regal eyes with a lorgnon suspended from an opulent moiré silk ribbon. This Benjamin was a sort of distant cousin several times removed, and so small and frail that it wouldn't be he who would make the branch of the genealogical tree sag as this leafless tree spreads out, rises and, above the circular human beings placed on the branches, the morning stars are singing with their horrible square open mouths. Benjamin's father's wife, with her pursed stuck-up lips, suffered her entire life because he would shave in the kitchen. He was a prosecutor and a small-time moneylender. In the vacant lot that ran alongside their garden, Benjamin would look for pots that he could use as tom-toms. 'A missionary? I'll disinherit you!' the juror-prosecutor would shout, his face raspberry coloured and his fist pounding the table. Benjamin the student missionary would take back the crumbs he had tossed to the birds of the sky; a big roof across from his window hid a celestial body behind its slate tiles; a fire would rage for a half-hour every day along that rooftop, a high virgin extending her chimney arms out to him. When he left for Africa, Eliza the missionary woman, leaning forward, was pacing up and down the deck of the ship, her black skirt dangling down too far here and there. They arrived at the Meschacebé River, for clothes a black woman was wearing a mere ostrich feather affixed to her waist, the muddy water of immense lakes would rise over the backs of strange beasts. Two years went by and

Benjamin, having returned to Europe, reached Fraidaigue, clasping under his arm a big book of African conversions which he hoped to sell off on them for the long winter evenings.

'If you wish me to stay,' he laughed—but Madame wasn't laughing and was staring at him—'if you wished me to stay, I'd like to remain for a while at Fraidaigue ... I mean, in the area. Oh, down there in Africa I have a well-stocked field of activities! ... I've just come from my sister-in-law's, the banker's wife. How she raises her children!'

He shuddered at the memory of the imitation Louis XIII armchairs beneath which the children would take shelter from their mother's whip. Alas, Benjamin realized he had fallen from Charybdis into Scylla! For at Fraidaigue, in the evenings, after the daily chores, Madame would sit on the red velvet settee, her eyes still concealed behind the lorgnon held in place by a moiré-silk ribbon lying across her harsh bosom; after sticking her knitting needle into the snowy constructions piled atop her head, she would take off the lorgnon, wipe it and, raising her regal eyes, choose someone at whom to stare. That evening, it was Benjamin. He grasped his balancing pole, rubbed his little feet in the chalk, edged his way along the tightrope. In vain. 'Yes,' he added with a muffled voice, 'yes, I have another brother, besides the banker. A gendarme. Yes.' And he fell off the tightrope. Madame kept staring at the wretched heap, travelling circus performers could be heard clanging their cymbals on the village square. Benjamin gathered up his few belongings and left, only to die a little later in the virgin forest.

'You see,' she was shouting. 'You see!' (It's the baroness who's shouting, the frightened villagers were murmuring. It's the baroness! What's the matter with her?) 'You see, Benjamin left without saying anything. It's César's fault! How will we ever marry Isabelle with that individual in the family?'

'And Julien, darling? I've always thought . . .'

'Julien? It's true I invited him to those garden balls I hosted for the village children. Those Venetian lanterns!'

She couldn't help but smile at the memory of those lanterns and, for a moment, her deep-sea-diver teeth could be seen.

'So you see, darling,' replied Eugène, rather reassured, 'that same Julien . . . Why wouldn't he marry Isabelle? He was here last night.'

'But you haven't understood anything! But you are . . .'

She was choking with rage.

'He's going away . . . for the entire summer . . . Will be a private tutor for those manufacturers. He's going away, are you listening? Answer instead of looking out the window!'

Watching the lake riddled with rain, Eugène grew silent. Rain again! On the vineyards! He could remain silent, experience had taught him that she wouldn't start hitting him. Indeed, while vigorously cleaning her fingernails, she began talking about hygiene. 'What a doctor I would have been! Those new discoveries . . . I could have directed, organized, lent a hand. Whereas here . . . ' She was staring at the wood-panelled grey walls, at the white-and-gold earthenware stove, at Eugène's obstinately turned back and, through the other window, at the lake, its grey hanging gardens. Terrified Benjamin left on his tiny chalk-rubbed feet; he got engaged to Eliza the missionary, a purple scarf hid her goitre, she had fallen from a window at the age of five and her left arm, withered above the elbow, remained attached to her body. 'Benjamin would have liked to marry me,' thought Isabelle while smiling with her too short lip. 'When a man brings you his theology thesis . . . I'm the one who didn't want him.' A stamp box hollowed out of bark, and shells, which are used as stitches down there, were the alluvial deposits left behind by Benjamin, who, moreover, was no longer called Benjamin but, rather, Dogodela, Small Stream. This is how he was christened by an African man who, in the neighbouring hut, was writing to his friends on a visiting card as big as a palm leaf: 'From today on, my name will no longer be Dogodela but, rather, *Urodonal*.' And he christened the little missionary with the name of Dogodela, for nothing is lost, nothing is created, as a professor who looked like Anatole France stated in 1910, nothing is lost, not even the names of dead girls who slowly fall to the ground like those shuttlecocks from yesteryear, their pink feathers stuck in a wax and velvet disk held in place by the gold-braided fastener that she would meticulously tack back down before throwing the shuttlecock back into our infantile hands. Dogodela had gone off to bring some medicine to a sick African woman who had a drowned look, her skin grey from fear and her stomach bloated; he pulled out a tick from his tiny thigh before penetrating into the forest, the big faces of the trees, their entangled limbs, welcomed him in, then closed behind him; try as he might to scatter crumbs behind him, the tiger gobbled them up in turn, he was never seen again. At the door of their hut, his big timid wife was waving, to no avail, the purple scarf that usually concealed her goitre; a scaly beast reared up its back in the muddy lake, causing high waves to rise despite the lack of wind. Poor Small Stream! Yet other suitors were on their way to Isabelle. Would Madame agree to mask her regal eyes with the lorgnon hanging in front of her ample bosom? Meanwhile, César the nomad, the D.P., kept leaving Fraidaigue, then returning to it, at each equinox. The three girl cousins, in fact handicapped by their rough-hewn pants tightened below each knee with a crocheted guipure, were engaged in a race to death. ('Soon, soon,' whispered Madame *with gusto*, 'a corpse at the neighbours'!') In the evening, the village's phosphorescent mirror image hovered in the sky, a hand arbitrarily set the limits of the lake, those two wild beasts, the water and the shore, trotting alongside each other, licking each other. Every spring, César would again find the bare earth of the vineyards: 'Earth! Earth!' he would shout, sitting on his small servant's wicker suitcase. As to the next suitor, Julien, the Creator's fingermark could still be seen on his flabby cheek. 'My young friend,' the pastor had said, his voice hissing between teeth worn down by preaching the Good Word, 'you'll be fine, you'll see, you'll be given all the latitude you need for your studies. Two girls need to be prepared for some vague exams, and one of them has to be treated tactfully, very much so.' Julien departed, dressed in black, his very high collar with its broken points wounding his bluish neck. Monsieur received him in a study as big as Europe; on the wall, all sorts of objects and animals crowded together:

cows, apples, a candlestick, a bit of tablecloth. Monsieur adjusted his monocle around his eye, a few remaining black hairs letting his scalp show through. Licking his index finger, he was leafing through *Mime Bathylle* which he had just received. 'Mornin', mornin',' he said to Julien while extending two fingers. A whole village of hens were being raised on the hill, Monsieur was mixing an egg cordial. His wife called the guests by clapping her hands. 'Bon appétit, ladies and gentlemen,' she said, sitting down. Across from Julien, one of those great beautiful creatures, who are born at the beginning of every century, was wearing a studded dog leash for a belt. 'I fear,' the mother said about the peas, 'that there was ... that there was a shurtage of vegetables this summer.' But was it really the schoolmistress' fault if Émile, the ward of the commune, would mumble *shurtage* and she didn't correct him? A blackbird was chirping on the plane tree, the grey branches of the lime tree were turning red, she secretly loved the mayor's son. And if lil' Émile read *shurtage*, this is because he was half-witted, he would head towards the front desk with his jerky gait, a patch on his rear, his frayed pants coming halfway up his legs, a little saliva at the corner of his purplish mouth, a half-witted boy in the depths of the deepest abodes of childhood. Lil' Émile would be mocked by the already convex girls strolling in great groups rocked by the wind, the long hair of one of them getting stuck in the apple core held by another. Émile spelt out *shurtage* aloud, and the schoolmistress heard nothing; with one foot forward, her hands crossed behind her back, dusty strands of hair falling down her nape, she was looking out the window at the motionless plane trees and the poplars letting their young reddish hair be blown along in the March wind; wisps of straw would suddenly fly up and dive back down in the air. She didn't correct *shurtage* but rapped on her desk and had them sing *Pretty May, pretty May* . . . Already deaf to this matter, Clotilde repeated *shurtage* till her last day. 'Mornin', mornin',' the financier would gracefully say whenever he met up with the little private tutor in the hallways of the castle. 'Mornin', mornin',' he called out rather impatiently and questioningly one morning when this little private tutor was standing, somewhat slumping, in the middle of the study as big as Europe. What, then, did he want? Naked beneath his dressing gown, the financier was licking his finger and leafing through Saint Thomas Aquinus' *Summa theologica*, which had been placed on a high oaken lectern. The sunlight was shining red and blue through the windows, the few transparent windowpanes were marked with the imperceptible graffiti of the prisoners, the beech and the mahogany trees were suffocating and screaming beneath the red rep petticoats with pompons, an enormous photograph of the grandfather showed none of the attributes, in his old idle hands, of the baker than he had been.

'M'sieur . . . ,' Julien was saying, slumping.

'What do you want, what do you want, my young friend?'

'I must say farewell to you, M'sieur.'

'But what's this, what's this? You were supposed to stay all summer long. Ah, how annoying. Has someone died? Is someone ill?'

'No, M'sieur, it's that I'm forced to leave.'

'Forced to leave? But why?'

'It's impossible for me to stay, I've already stayed too long.'

The watering can struck a spade, Jämes was pushing the lawnmower, the fresh hairs of the lawn leaping up and scattering in the mild air. Hearing the noise of the water spurting up from the fountain, Julien vigorously chased away the thought of Isabelle. Oh, couldn't that moribund little private tutor leave? He who needed to finish reading the *Summa theologica* of Saint Thomas Aquinas before lunch!

'I've stayed too long for my tranquillity,' continued Julien, sweating, the broken points of his collar wounding the bluish flesh of his neck.

'You see, it's because I love Mademoiselle, your daughter.'

'Oh, how unpleasant, how unpleasant! And which of my two daughters, please?'

Alas, Eugénie was too beautiful, it was poor little Mathilde whom he proposed to marry . . . The father approached and furiously grasped his shoulder, felt the flabby white flesh underneath the black clothes and then stepped back, impotently. He told him to leave and pack up.

'So the young man,' said the father while sitting down on the chair upholstered with green foliage, 'your young man is leaving, going away, he can't stay, you'll never guess the reason. And you first of all, how much have you studied? Up to the Pharaohs? But then why is it he doesn't have you read *Thaïs*? What a Frenchman! What a genius! Ah, if the people here only read him . . .'

One day while he was walking between the henhouses, he heard a child shouting, 'Wait and see!' See what, little boy? The child was walking barefoot in the mud, his mother was a widow and a day labourer, he sent them a little book: *Say . . . Don't Say . . .* 'Say: a portion of Agen plum pie.' He packaged it carefully, the sharp angles, recalling the days when, as a herbalist's helper, he would wrap up herb teas, smoothing out the paper, tying up the package with string from a ball spinning in its box, his clothes smelling of sweet clover, the herbalist, who was the friend of princes, would send overseas those packages of tea harvested in the country of Edom, all the inhabitants, and first and foremost the priest, receiving them once a year, the children running alongside the procession through the mud puddles where they would disturb the salamander hurriedly scampering off for the princely wedding, but, alas, the whole procession vanished into a iron-rail fence in *trompe l'oeil*, and he, the young helper left behind in the shop, would go from the chamomile room to the centaury room, and then to the sage room, using the master's scissors to etch the prisoners' graffiti onto the windowpane tinted blue because of the herbs.

'Anatole France! What beautiful French! *That's* a genius for you!'

He was gazing at his plump little hands placed on the edge of the table.

'But *Daddy* . . . '

'Ah, yes, I forgot . . . The little private tutor. You'll never guess why he's leaving. It's that he loves, lovvves, one of you.'

Poor little Mathilde placed her hand on her heart and tried to raise her face shaped like a square shovel on which pimples moved around every day like stars.

Eugénie started laughing. The mother's double chins were resting on a bosom kept violently high by means of a corset that compressed her breasts which would be able to fall back down only in the evening; the worn-out corset would then lie atop a green rep chair across which lay an embroidered band of cloth that had come from the grandmother, a washwoman who, with her wrinkled hand extending from the end of her white-velvet-covered arm, was pensively bringing to her damp mouth a bit of melon stuck on the tip of a knife.

'He said he loved, he lovvved . . . can you believe it . . . '

'But *Daddy*,' said beauteous Eugénie, 'I assure you that I never encouraged him. Never. Oh, I of course noticed . . . '

She was raising her hand and softly nodding 'no'.

'But this is about Mathilde,' he finally yelled.

Eugénie jumped up and ran off, pushing aside the big tapestry that they had had no qualms about hanging in front of the supplies room and that was playing hot cockles with its leaf-like hands. The father led Mathilde into his study, lit up a cigar, giving a few little taps to his velvet coat from which dust was already flying up; the ceiling with its golden caissons was imperceptibly coming down towards his pink-and-black head. 'What? You love him? But you're kidding, my daughter. Look, all this belongs to you.' He opened the stained-glass windows, pointed to the hills covered with henhouses resembling a series of wardrobe closets on piles; the hens were strolling about in groups, only Fanchon had broken away and was dreamily pecking about at invisible things in the freshly overturned earth that expected a corpse per minute and that was going to be frustrated with Abraham, falling from the cornice at this very instant, for he weighs so little that, dropping into the void because César, the evening before—the messenger had seen him—had removed a stone beneath the painted window, comes right back up and is returned to human beings even as the enchanted hoop rolled by Armand onto the terrace would come back all by itself, towards the children.

'It's for you,' he continued, 'that I constructed all this . . . all this business.'

'But Papa, I love him.'

'Ah, but what's love, what's love?'

Julien was packing his luggage in the garret, where a small Eiffel tower stood on his table, a souvenir offered by Monsieur Eiffel himself who had come to visit and had left with his pockets full of egg cordial. An elegant iron construction with a swan neck supported a beard-shaving plate. Suddenly Mathilde came in, struggling to lift her pimple-covered face; a heavy hand was pressing down on her neck.

'My father told me . . . You're leaving?'

'I'm obliged to leave.'

'But why?'

'I told him I was suffering too much.'

'But from what?'

Why was she pretending not to understand? For a moment, he wished to stop talking, to keep piling into his suitcase his shirts and those dangerous celluloid collars that catch on fire from candle flames, cigars, sparks from hooves; travellers found nothing better to do than jump into the lake to put out their enflamed collars. On August nights, from Fraidaigue, such flame trails could be seen. Julien unpacked his luggage, that evening Mathilde sat on the arm of his armchair, smoking a cigarette, blowing the smoke towards the ceiling from the corner of her mouth, calling Julien 'My Little Love'.

'Monsieur,' he asked, 'have you read Auguste Comte? No? You haven't?'

Nodding in approval, Mathilde, her eyes tearful, her lips half-parted, wasn't listening to her father telling her that it was time to go to bed, that it was past eight and that she would otherwise stay up restless half the night once again. She went upstairs only when her sister did. 'The reign of the close-cropped lamb is over,' she said curtly in the stairway. Julien left the next morning, rang at the tower door, lil' Benjamin had just collected his few things and returned to his well-stocked field of activities. 'Julien!' exclaimed Isabelle, sliding over to open the parlour door. Julien would like to marry me, but do I want him? Julien sat down on the velvet settee, Semiramis seemed about to smile, her deep-sea-diver teeth could already be seen; hanging down in front of the window, the gardens full of pale-blue flowers were sparkling in the April sunlight. She looks satisfied today, the villagers were whispering, she's neither groaning nor sneezing. So much the better for our windows.

Had Julien already come back? Had anyone really imagined he'd stay six months down there? He smiled, showing his yellow teeth. It's because something had happened, something fortunate. 'Fortunate for me.'

Madame looked him over closely, first his nose, then her eyes descended to his bluish neck wounded by the broken points of the collar. He raised his hand to his neck; a brand-new ring shining on his finger; the copper door of the stove and the window catch were also glaring unbearably.

'Actually, I've become engaged . . . to the director's daughter.'

Isabelle was leaning so heavily on the fireplace that the joints of her fingers whitened, as did those of Gwen

34

leaning against the wall covered with moss and maidenhair fern when she understood that César wouldn't marry her and she resigned herself to leaving with Fritz, who had recently donned his military corset.

'The director's daughter? Which one? Eugénie?'

'No. The younger one. Oh, she's several years younger, the little one. I'm marrying the young one. We'll be getting married soon.'

'Close that window!' she was shouting, 'This spring sunlight is giving me a headache.'

Meanwhile, Julien was explaining that, when he had arrived down there, a carriage was waiting for him at the train station, he had come across Eugénie riding in her brougham, the driver sitting next to her, she had taken the whip and given him a friendly wave, Monsieur had welcomed him as a guest; he served more as a secretary, they would read Saint Thomas Aquinas' *Summa theologica* together. The couple would go to live in Italy, Paris, Heidelberg. Then he would enter the factory as an associate, naturally as a lawful partner. 'My theology will be very useful to me.' Madame asked again if those young girls had ever done logarithms, Julien answered no, and took his leave. In Venice on the canal, Mathilde, her eyes gleaming, her lips half-parted, was listening to the mediocre serenade. They were staying at the Danieli. 'Poor aunt Emma,' Julien sometimes murmured, 'dying in Venice, drowning when that boat capsized.' On the Lido, he ran into Madame, who was gazing at the sea, and Eugène, standing behind her, rocking back and forth between the heels and tiptoes of his shoes. Will I find my embassy attaché tomorrow in Torcello, Madame was musing, after all these years? They each shook Julien's limp hand. He said he was staying at the Danieli. Mathilde was resting in her room; he kept her away from any overexcitement; they had a suite at the Danieli. 'I would so much have liked to marry a poor girl,' he said after some silence. And he entered the Danieli.

Meanwhile, with the coming of spring, a strangely feverish César was leaving the Maison d'En Haut and looking forward to seeing the naked pale purplish earth of the first vineyard; standing at the bottom of the avenue, Mélanie, watching him vanish, placed her hand on her tumultuous breasts. Squatting in front of the emerald-green faience stove, all sisterly affection done away with and dressed in the white gown of insane women, Zoé was warming her fingers, with their overgrown nails, for the last time that season. When César leaves, this means that winter has given way, that the osier bushes are reddening at the edges of the streams, that the whole world is taking on the smell of stables and manure. Leaning against the doorframe, the little manservant of the Maison d'En Haut was breathing easy; from now until autumn, the bruises left by Monsieur César's blows would have time to fade away. Mélanie went to clean the stables of Augeas and stopped on the threshold. The angle shelf was holding up a cast-iron snake-shaped candlestick, a grimy cup, some leftover wine turned oily in a thick green bottle, a broken part of which showed a secret whiteness. Did he drink? He sometimes reeled when he left the stable. She picked up the glass and, stealthily, swigged the bitter, oily dregs. The horse was stamping at the straw, she thought of those fabulous beasts of her childhood when she would stand at the front door of her house and, through the fog, horses would loom between the earth and the sky.

'But Fraidaigue is only a great big country mansion, not a château,' she was saying that same evening. And the tower, what is it, would you please let me know? Our neighbour Joseph Dimanche—how he built a tower! Narrow at the bottom, bulging out at the top, now that was a tower!

With the edge of his hand, Adolphe was raking in the crumbs on the table. 'Why,' he wondered distractedly, 'amass treasures on this earth?'

'Moreover, at the time of Their Excellences, it was a mere granary . . . All the same, we could have had one of your vineyards because your brother had the château. The château,' she repeated pompously.

All it was, actually, was a great big country mansion, you couldn't say it was a real château.

'If at least the other tower were still standing. Yet I wonder, even so, by what right did your brother get this "château"?'

'Because he's the eldest son, I suppose.'

'The eldest? But what about César?'

'Oh, César . . . '

César has left for six months, it's spring, the ward of the commune is breathing easy, but only autumn, which brings César back, tastes like springtime for Mélanie. Leaving the Maison d'En Haut, where one needs a pocket compass to know where east and west lie, he was heading down towards Fraidaigue; there, every morning, the dazzling south rises from the water. He stopped at the bend in the road and sat down on his small wicker suitcase bound with a rope. The lake was barely quivering under the weight of motionless fishing boats. Back from Italy, Madame realized spring had returned. Even people with no memories know so immediately; even the poor half-wits of the asylum lift their gummy eyes to the sky, their purplish mouths drooling with saliva. After the Venetian palaces, Madame found Fraidaigue seemingly diminished by a third. 'Has César arrived?' she asked. 'Apparently no shouts can yet be heard coming from the stable. Ah, he's our cross! But let's not judge, as your brother Adolphe says. That fellow's a real imbecile.' Meanwhile, César was reaching the village, walking down the street where ancient waves had modelled houses into their inverted images, and he emerged in the gardens of Fraidaigue. 'Who in hell put the wood like this?' he muttered. He put down his wicker suitcase, pushed his hat back on his head and began to kick at the dead wood. 'There he is,' whispered Madame, standing at the window, hugging to her bosom the black velvet palatine that was giving off a draft of cold air. 'Is it you, César, making all that racket?' Without replying, he left the courtyard and went down to the beach. The fishermen had just snared a Roman vase in their nets and were bringing it to the château even though only one tower was left. The other tower can still be heard shivering when the easterly Vaudaire wind blows. 'But if he demanded that the property be shared out,' said Eugène, painted by Raphaël with one of those big rosy, regular-featured, boring faces. 'If he got married? That is, if he remarried and if this time . . . What would we have to do? Sell the château? Or pay a mortgage every year? And with what? For this reason, darling, don't get him worked up.' 'Oh,' he added in haste, seeing his wife slowly turning around, 'of course it's not you who . . . '

'Me? I get him worked up!'

'No, no, darling, don't put yourself into such a state. No, everything is his fault. He doesn't know how to acknowledge what we do for him . . . '

'Put up, fed, six months here, six months there,' she was saying dreamily. 'How he lives in clover! With only his life insurance to pay. Ah, he's our cross! How will we ever get Isabelle married?'

Had he at least said good morning to them? No, he was cursing at the pile of wood. And when they went to church on Sundays, he would bring shame on them. 'Always walking behind us, wearing that old velvet coat.' That is, he would try to step on Madame's shadow, after avoiding the one cast by the demolished tower from which the turtledove had fallen while trying to pick some maidenhair fern. 'Look, he's left his suitcase standing there on the terrace. I bet he's already lying on the beach.' She majestically strolled through the house. Lying on the beach, César was joyfully feeling the naked earth sagging beneath his weight; he was fingering a few pink and grey pebbles that the March waves had washed ashore and gazing at the sky speckled with blue windows and angels in *trompe l'oeil*. He was thinking of the November firmament, more in keeping with his wretched life, those curtains that slowly open onto a dark-tinged sky across which a solitary bird is flying, sticking out its long neck. An idle wasp emerging from the winter darkness was lingering on the beach, the spheres were likewise lingering on the threshold, warming themselves in the first sunlight of the world before flying heavily upwards, their legs sticky, in order to take up their positions in the universe. When César stood up, he reeled, staggering like a drunken bird, confounding east and west, past and future. 'He drinks,' Madame was muttering. That evening the nomad, the D.P., was edging his way along the cornice, his nightshirt flapping about his red-haired legs; he was himself going to consolidate the stone beneath the painted window. The next two windows belong to the room in which he watched her dying on her bed, after he had elbowed his way through a crowd of strangers. Are the children grouped around her there? For there is no resemblance between us and them, Eugène with his big rosy face, giving a thump to his brother: 'As long as I live, there'll always be a bowl of soup for you,' Adolphe already bald, his eyes weary and wrinkled behind his lorgnon, Zoé gone mad in order to escape insulting pity, César whose carrot-red hairs have been sewn one by one to a felt disk. But they're not dead, one would have known so if they were, where are the children? Since César's room has only one curtain, the other one having been stolen by the messenger who henceforth dressed in green—why didn't they ever let her approach the turtledove?—he sleeps little, for the lake is vaguely phosphorescent at night, and he slumbers by day in the stable, his head leaning on the flank of Jenny who suddenly starts moving like an entire world and goes rolling through the universe. Whenever he awoke, swearing and shouting would immediately be heard, the servant lad dashing out of the stable. During this time, Eugène placed on his desk one of those paper boats that the young Venetian servant woman made with menus in order to entertain a child of the sea and that she would launch with her firm brown arm onto the lagoon. He had kept it hidden in the lining of his boater during the entire trip. 'You'll never know how to make a boat like this,' he said, pointing his chin at it. Madame stood up slowly. But it was only to retort, 'Does that servant woman perhaps know anything about logarithms?' In her absurd village of clock-makers, where every man had a telescope screwed on beneath his eyebrow and where the visitors from the Franche-Comté would arrive breathless on Sundays with a fourfold butter cake in a grey canvas bag, she would speak about logarithms to Eugène, who had proposed to her on the very next day after the ball, and when the doctor came to Fraidaigue to deliver Abraham, she was holding the little green book of logarithms, her finger placed on page 50. 'The baby is doing well,' he said in the next-door house, which belonged to Rose who, despite her liver pains, could still give orders to the servant woman leaning against the doorframe, yawning, and scratching her armpit by thrusting her hand inside the neckline of her blouse. 'The baby is doing well, we'll tell her his name is Abraham, we can see she's not used to babies, she'd prefer doing logarithms.' The servant gossiped about all this in the kitchen, and the poor aged woman, who would drag herself along in her heel-worn flat shoes while carrying the newspaper and would mend old clothes in the evening in order to give them to mothers with lots of children, picked up a plant thrown out in the rubbish behind Fraidaigue and placed it, in front of her garret window, on that sheet-metal gutter where pigeon feet sounded like hail; when the plant flowered, the old woman saw it as a logarithm. From her tiny window she could see a fragment of the lake; with a few flaps of its wings, a bird was heading for Fraidaigue, Madame watching it carefully. How animals loved her! Coming back from the village and still wearing his hat, Eugène shouted: 'Old Élise is ill!' Madame did not turn around. 'Old Élise is ill, she's got bronchopneumonia. Let's hope she's not playing the empress any more!' Her head bowed, Isabelle was learning how to do needle lace. 'What,' the interned French officer had said the evening before, tall like Pepin the Short and with a handsome pointed derrière below his blue tunic, 'you don't do needle lace? At home, all the young girls . . . '

'Old Élise is suffocating, they're bringing oxygen bottles to her,' exclaimed Eugène as he came back in that evening. She was suffocating in her little room that was itself having difficulty breathing, most of its space being taken up by a big, high, cherry-wood bed. 'Be brave, you'll get better,' the corset salesman was saying, all the while sewing up a maternity girdle near her bed. He composed such pretty advertising ditties for his girdles and corsets! But she looked him over closely, he dropped a piece of pink satin, sweat beading on his forehead. When Eugène returned home the next evening, he cried out, trembling while hanging his boater on the hat-peg, 'Old Élise has passed away. Dead women tell no tales.' Madame kept trying to stare him down, in vain: he dared to go back out and stroll along the beach with César, their arms around each other's shoulders. The next day, the mountains suddenly appeared closer and blue-green. It was almost chilly in the garden where Eugène was following Madame around, carrying plants in a newspaper torn open in spots. 'A few days ago,' he said, 'I planted a pelargonium in this flowerbed.' 'Oh,' he added hastily, 'I can remove it if you think . . . Beginning tomorrow, I'm going to get up an hour earlier and work in the garden.'

'Yes,' she said, 'yes, Eugène.'

Eugène raised his axe and knocked her down dead. The next morning, he got up at the usual hour, finding the lunch tablecloth folded over his plate and Madame ostentatiously sweeping the parquet with her walled-up-woman's big, beautiful, lividly white hands. Old Élise's corpse was still lying on her cherry-wood bed! She was waiting for Madame in vain; it was only much later that César removed a board from the bottom of *Danae* and invited Madame to go fishing. Like today, a storm was approaching, that day, a big bird was gliding above Fraidaigue, flapping its wings towards Italy, then flying back into the Jura skies, from which it flew down once again over the local area. 'But how strange it is,' Madame was muttering, standing at her window, 'animals love me. Jenny, for instance, in the stable! And sometimes swans accompany me. And the other day, a flock of gulls flew over my head.' As she was leaning out to watch the unknown bird, she noticed a suitor for Isabelle coming down from the train station. It was Pepin the Short marching hurriedly forward in his Sambre-and-Meuse Army pace, all waxed up, his back arched, a handsome pointed derrière below his blue tunic. 'I could marry him,' Isabelle was musing by the very next day. 'When a man speaks to you about his aunt, the Baroness of Sainte-Amélie, who was killed in the Passy church on Good Friday, about his mother, about his house near Saint-Maclou, and if he says: "Don't you do needle lace, Mademoiselle Isabelle? At home, all the young girls do ... "' But go and live in a garrison town? She nonetheless applied herself to learning how to do needle lace and embroidered so much, indeed so much, that the man from the canton of Uri and Dogodela had to draw apart the needle-lace pieces dangling down everywhere in order to go over to her. As an imprisoned young soldier, Pepin had lived in the shade of the lime tree of Frau von Kleist's salon in Potsdam. He cultivated the general's garden. Many years beforehand, Frau von Kleist had left in a vase a seed sent to her by her cousin, the Baroness Hilda, a completely pallid woman who lived in Bamberg, hoping for a suitor. The lime tree grew, reached a metre and a half in height, its growth would have been halted at that point in Switzerland, in France, in Italy; two metres, Berta von Kleist propped it up with a stake, the emperor was talking about keeping his powder dry. The lime tree measured two and a half metres, she had it climb up the wall, the sails kept passing by along the sandy grounds of Brandenburg; three and a half metres, four metres, military inspections were taking place on the seas. The lime tree went through the ceiling, came back down on the other side, the emperor declared war. Frau Oberhofgärtner, who had come with her Putti to have a cup of coffee, was speaking French to

Pepin and wearing a large velvet beret. Every morning she would dive into the Spree and swim solemnly, her shoulders above the water, her head covered with a large rubber cap. In April, when the white sails once again began fleeing across the ground, Pepin managed to get himself replaced by a Junker, he vanished into the morning haze, Frau von Kleist secretly wept, the bones of her corset visible beneath her green dress with guipures. Pepin crossed the border, the cherry trees were in bloom around a reddish city, suddenly the countryside emerged, the rivers turned green, white and colder, black boulders were being born amid the foam, the fountainhead of the world. The train was running past lakes that were being led, borne along, by streams. Pepin hopped off onto the platform and, straightening his small body, began marching forward in his Sambre-et-Meuse Army pace. After arriving at the village, he settled into the count's room in which the Venetian curtains formerly held up by angels were still hanging and in which the motionless count was trying to wear down the twins' patience. The green, fragrant April wind was blowing over meadows that were yellow only yesterday. César was shouting in the depths of the stable. 'Peasant!' muttered Pepin. In the shadows, he could only indistinctly make out César, dressed in tawny velvet, his coat trimmed with the braids that one makes with a pitchfork along the manure pile on

Sundays. 'Peasants!' Steam would blow from César's nostrils when he left the stable, he usually lived in the depths of this warm abode, the past legible to him in the tawny liquid manure. 'Where are the children?'

'Listen. He's beating that little manservant again. What a cross! Oh, he's my cross. And you, you shut up. I beg you to stop repeating that he could claim his share. Six months here, six months there! And with the way his marriage ended, he's not going to start all over again, say what you like. Providence exists after all. Now keep your mouth shut, here's that French officer.'

As the horse César was leading to the fountain trotted over the cobblestones, sounding like a man hurrying along with hobnailed shoes, Pepin, ushered into the parlour, was almost struck by the red-and-blue gentleman framed in fine gold who resembled him so, and he half drew out his riding whip. Isabelle appeared, bending her knees, for she was too tall for both Pepin and Dogodela; they had look up into her nostrils. Travelling across France, Pepin's mother was getting ever nearer to him in a train crowded with goateed gentlemen and farmers carrying covered baskets with goosenecks sticking out. From her bag, she brought out bobbins and bobbins of thread that she kept biting off with her lovely French teeth. 'My dear daughter,' she asked Isabelle the next day, 'is it true you don't know how to do needle lace?'

Isabelle protested in vain that she in fact knew how to do Reticella, English embroidery, Venetian needle lace, Bologna needle lace and Richelieu needle lace. Pepin's mother wasn't listening.

'What? You don't even know how to tie a fisherman's knot? My dear child!'

She was sticking her needle in and out of the yellow homespun mesh on her knee and embroidering a bird resembling the one that for centuries had been perched on a stone shoulder polished by the rains, ever full of rainbows, of the Île-de-France.

'When the children were small,' Madame was explaining, 'we'd host garden balls with Venetian lanterns.'

Pepin was talking to Isabelle on the balcony, the lake was dully thudding against the shore, no one seemed to be listening to it except the stranger sitting at a table on the inn terrace and watching the visitors from the Franche-Comté, with a fourfold butter cake in their grey canvas bag, hurrying onward at the news of Abraham's fall. So many times César had removed a stone from the cornice beneath the painted window and then returned at night to replace it, his nightshirt floating around his red-haired legs! So many times he had urged Abraham to get on board the lifeboat in order to save *The Eagle*! He would then run down the beach: 'Come back, Abraham! Come back! It's me, Uncle César!' But the lifeboat was already cleaving through the waves.

'Paris!' Pepin was saying to Isabelle, Paris, its bridges rimmed with spirits standing on golden spheres reflected in the Seine and, like a mirage, in the grey sky! As the train arrives, searching for its track among a thousand tracks, changing tracks, jolting, jerking to the side, the city alights on the earth. Isabelle was musing absentmindedly that, in Rome, it's the aqueducts and triumphal arches straight ahead that create a big construction in the air. I could have married that Italian count, didn't I often spot him at his window, the one looking down on the lane where Ol' Miss Gibaude has her house? So pale, so immense, he would stand there watching me, with those sparrows in the folds of his waistcoat; and when the twins led him away, he lifted his eyes as he passed near the gate. He would have liked to have her, it's she who didn't want him.

'Back home in Rouen,' he was saying, 'we live near Saint-Maclou, there's perhaps not much sunlight but the house is big and beautiful, and there's an apple orchard out back. My nanny . . .'

His trousers were making a noise like insect wings. 'But Mum,' Isabelle was saying, 'he tells me all about his life, school, the schoolteacher who doesn't believe in God and has an ink stain at the tip of her pointed nose, the hen-shaped yew trees in their garden. The army, Mum, that's what is best in France.' Out of respect for Isabelle, Madame decided to stop staring at Pepin's mother, who was holding the needle lace mesh on her knees, she sat there motionless as a stone, looking with love at her small-sized son with his nifty uniform like a red-and-blue insect, just like those she would send to heaven with a flick of her fingers whenever a regal, severe Saint Gabriel the Angel was in the neighbour-hood: Burnet, burnet, go tell the Good Lord to make the weather beautiful tomorrow so it won't rain down on my stone head. What trouble she had getting her thirteenth-century turban made by that woman milliner with a moustache and a lorgnon, who lived in a two-room flat stinking of glue and rice pudding! As to Madame, she now wore only one type of hat, which recalled the one Mary Stuart wore, entirely brimmed with a mourning veil: one never knows . . . Mélanie would surely die out of heartbreak, as well as the three girl cousins engaged in a race to the death in their little house near Vieux-Collège . . . 'Yet the army,' Isabelle kept repeating in the parlour, 'that's what is best in France.' Alas, Mme Scaramache suddenly dragged her son away! The last glimpse that Isabelle caught of him, at that bend in the wall where the useless maidenhair fern grows, was his handsome pointed derrière sticking out below his blue tunic. 'He'd have liked to marry me,' she kept softly saying in the parlour. But after returning from the grocery shop in the lane, where she had bought some peppercorns, she discovered that the puppies had been nibbling at her needle-lace albums; she was able to save only half a rose, the wheels of a god's chariot and the neck of a guitar. Night was falling. An invisible flute in his fingers, Abraham was hunched up against the window, seemingly ready to fly off into the night; deformed Ulysse was sitting in a wicker armchair, his wimpy leg positioned on an inclined stool embroidered with a doe, and cleaning his fingernails. And César? He seems to be secretly removing a board from the bottom of *Danae*. 'Upon my word, doesn't it seem,' his brother Eugène was saying while he was still living, that is, before a spider dashed up from violet-strewn waters and left a purple mark on his face as he was sleeping on that wooden balcony where he could escape from Madame's staring, 'doesn't it seem César is removing a board from the rowboat?' Would he invite Madame to go fishing? For the time being, she was standing motionlessly on that balcony that recedes against the backdrop of the waves, and her walled-up-woman's long lividly white hands were hanging straight down her sides because she kept herself from touching anyone with her arms or hips, knowing all her energy would immediately vanish as if from an electric shock. Except, of course, those dear brave dead ones who could be fondled and embraced at ease. 'Mmmm . . . how good it is,' she would say, just as soon turning back on the threshold to return and embrace the corpse. But corpses don't show up very often when families are at peace. This is why she was attentively awaiting the demise of one of those three girl cousins who lived together and who, indeed, were engaged in a race to the death. Would it be Billie with her lilac-coloured detachable collar and, whenever she turns her head, that face as forgettable as the vague features of the moon; or bad-tempered Adeline who looks like a Sioux with her big flat blotchy cheeks and her knitting needle stuck through her muddy chignon; or Charlotte with her shiny greasy face and whose Boyard footsteps cave in the floorboards? Billie was the last of the three to arrive in Vieux-Collège; what the two other cousins spotted getting out of the mail coach was a whisky-stained pigskin suitcase, tied-up boxes, and then Billie and her false lilac-coloured collar, and just as soon as she had turned back to grab her toilet case, they had already forgotten her face, her nose, her mouth, all those vague features of the moon. As to Charlotte, she turned up with still-fuming goatskin trunks, her mighty footsteps bringing her from the mail coach to the house, all the while caving in the courtyard cobblestones; hard of hearing, she would jump whenever someone suddenly spoke to her from too close up. 'Here I am!' Adeline would shout during those first weeks of milk and innocence when paradise begins again; in the evening, Billie would find Charlotte's panther-skin hot water bottle in her bed. Alas, it took them little time to ask sly questions about Anatole—'Charlotte, haven't you received any news from your son?'—and to put blatantly on the round table, for Billie, the Exuber Bust Developer Method. (For did Billie use, yes or no, hemp-tow falsies instead of breasts?) 'My liver is bickering with me,' one of them would say, 'this is my last Christmas.' 'Oh, you'll bury us all,' the other would retort. And the two of them couldn't keep themselves from sneaking a glance at Charlotte's flabby stomach; she had borne a child. How heavy that must be! And to come out through such a tiny opening! One moonlit evening, Billie went out without wearing a coat to fetch some milk with her purplish woody hands. Charlotte waddled fast and heavy after her, loosening the cobblestones along the way, and forcefully placed on her cousin's shoulders—how skinny she was!—her own Boyard coat that was moth-eaten even before the countess had tossed it to her after rummaging in a chest as big as a whole region of Europe, nothing but her big Russian derrière with its thousands of fatty folds showing as she threw furs and woollens down to the governesses standing in a row at the bottom of the staircase, and when she turned around, her poppy-red, terribly wrinkled face could be seen, she dealt out two or three more slaps and sat down to drink some black tea. As she waited for her milk, the coat made Billie sweat so much she caught a chill. 'I met those refugees, those Russians,' she said to Charlotte upon returning. 'How dirty they are!' 'The dirtiest, most ignorant people of Europe,' stated Adeline, going even further. 'You have no idea . . . ,' muttered Charlotte softly. 'You have to have lived that life in order to understand . . . Those clear nights . . . ' And Wladimir calling out to her under the aspens and stretching out his arms! 'You have no idea . . . You have to have lived over there. We'd go to bed only towards morning.' 'A lazy people,' snorted Adeline while adjusting her stocking heel and sticking a needle in her chignon. 'That's where you picked up those habits, Charlotte.' She would stay in bed all morning long, a panther-skin hot water bottle on her stomach. Adeline would choose this very moment to make noise by roasting coffee on the common stove where they heated water on Saturday evenings, one after the other washing their stiff, greenish, bruised legs. Adeline would loudly churn the coffee in the roaster, the early-morning smell of Europe drifting out of the house and going over to the Russian refugees tramping along the road with their pointed beards and slanting eyes, with those rope scars on their necks, their big pointed stomachs beneath black clothing showing the marks of barbed wire and lands where oats sprout up in a few enchanted days. 'I think I have bronchitis,' said Billie while touching her right side with an imponderable hand. 'One doesn't die from it, you'll bury us all.' Offended, Billie went back up to her room; as a young child, she had been locked up in boarding schools full of lightweight cane chairs—at every window, a Jewish girl with a low forehead was studying the sky and birds of passage flying in triangular formations. But was Billie in fact dying before the others? The doctor in his little mustard-yellow coat had to be fetched; he left his wife, who was twice as tall and heavy as he was and kept setting upon the world her eyes filled with the Sehnsucht of obese women recalling the days when they would swim around in water by giving big flaps with their tails. Rumblings could be heard in Billie's stomach, she vomited up an eleven-inch tapeworm, the edifice of her life was collapsing, did she still have a body beneath her grey silk robe? So much care taken, her whole life long, to slip on her nightshirt while her cheek was holding down her day shirt, unbuttoned beforehand, on her shoulder. That evening, she let her rice pudding cool down in the chipped bowl. Would she feed those worms that quickly swam to the right, to the left, and whose noise filled the room? Never! 'Hey!' Adeline was saying in the kitchen, shaking her copper pot with a handle so long that it was lying on the teakettle's shoulder, 'It's not me who would have wanted a man!' Fat Charlotte, sitting at the table, was silently wiping away a drop of grease trickling down her chin. 'And a child! It's not me who would have wanted a child. For the way they remain attached to you . . . You tire yourself out raising them, and then . . . Charlotte, haven't you received any news from Anatole?'

With her toothless gums, Adeline was chewing on an old walnut that she had picked up in the orchard and smashed open against the stone cistern. Charlotte was going down into the orchard, the chilly black east wind biting, for a while, her podgy face with its grey bangs. Sniggering, Adeline was turning around to take her handkerchief from inside her faille bag that was hanging on the back of her chair. Meanwhile, Billie was very ill; she had vomited up a second tapeworm. 'She's listening to herself,' Adeline was muttering while making a din wiping the dishes. Did she have, or not, hemp-tow falsies instead of breasts? Élise's daughter Little Marie, who was taking care of her—who will pay for all this, may I ask?—was attempting to hold Billie down on the bed by pressing hard on her bony knees that kept trying to rise and curl back onto her bosom. Lying sideways on her pillows, dripping with sweat, she was recalling those Spanish Bourbons who no longer had anything on their land but bushes and a quart of water per day and per person to drink and wash themselves with, and those grey-green mornings in Scotland when pikes swam off with Sir Harry and, all the while turning around and glancing over their shoulders, dragged him, his hat pushed back on his head, so harshly up North that he never returned. Her grey hair rolling back and forth over the pillow, she is now turning her face, which little Marie forgets just as soon, towards the faded flowers on the wall. Once one had stopped looking at that face, one would forget it like the moon's face, its nose and mouth having turned into clouds. 'But this is impossible, doesn't she want to die?' Adeline gets up at the first sting of dawn even as César, having just arrived at Fraidaigue in April, stays up for nights on end whenever the vineyard runs the risk of freezing.

'She's sleeping,' said little Marie, her own head drooping in fits and starts onto her bosom. But she was dead, emptied of her scanty substance. Tipped off who knows how, Madame—'A dead woman!' they were shouting, 'a dead woman in the neighbourhood!'— came dashing across the puddles. Adeline was getting dressed in a hurry, putting on her corset with its breast pockets. Billie . . . She was trying hard not to wonder whether Billie had, or had not, hemp-tow falsies instead of breasts; she slipped on her pantaloons with those crocheted lace tighteners below the knees, three petticoats, her Sunday dress, and here's old mother Gaspard standing at the top of the wooden staircase up which Madame, weeping, is climbing. Oh, Billie, Billie, her lilac-coloured detachable collar! Oh my Billie! She's dead. And to say that only yesterday I was speaking to her. I. That I was handing her a verbena cutting. Oh, she didn't know anything about taking care of plants! But she's dead. And to say that only yesterday . . . Oh my Billie! Her strong white hand is gripping the banister polished by dozens of dead women's hands; this is where, at night, the great uncle met up with his sister's shade coming down to the kitchen to drink one last glass of water. 'So, Billie,' Madame declared somewhat breathlessly, 'is no more. The first of the three to go.' Adeline suddenly swallowed her saliva. 'You see, when she complained, it wasn't for nothing.' I don't want Madame touching me, when she walks by, with those hips that bore children! Madame's harsh bosom nonetheless grazed Adeline's skinny bosom, they both thought they were going to faint, as they had long ago amid the circus crowd while they were gazing at Queen Mab standing on a top with her pointed head and ridiculous crown, and at those Siamese twins joined by a strip of flesh. The onlookers massing and squeezing together were holding one another up, one's personal force fading away because of the unsettling physical contacts. Everyone kept secretly putting his hand to his side, thinking that a fleshy arm was coming out of his heart. 'She didn't suffer, she didn't sense she was dying,' Adeline and Charlotte were claiming. Madame slowly approached Billie, kissed her cheek. Somewhere in the room rose the moon that shines on the faces of the newly dead lying on their last beds. Standing out enormous, yellow and detached from the sky, the earth's moon was shining behind the sequoia. Madame was kissing with delight the icy flesh, walking away, then returning just after arriving at the threshold. 'One more time,' she would whisper, 'one more time!' She had forced her way into Élise's room when she had been lying enthroned and enormous on her cherry-wood bed and had kissed her some twenty times. But she had to resign herself to leaving Billie; alas, there were not many corpses left on the horizon, she could count the future family deaths on her fingers: perhaps Mélanie would die out of heartbreak, Eugène whose eyes and swollen feet presaged nothing good—she didn't even foresee the spider that would dash up from the violet-strewn lake. The last boat wailed, it was the black breeze, frost would fall on their vineyards tonight. 'Where's César, where's your brother?' she groaned when she found Eugène in the parlour. Where was César? At the fair? He was courting that shooting-gallery woman, but no, he wasn't courting her, he was strolling behind the fabric shops with the curator's niece, the engineer's daughter, but no, not at all, he was entering L'Ancre to have a drink, he was flying off on his bicycle to reach the country of the Lowlands. 'Oh, it's too much, I feel it, here'—she was touching her earth-sized head—'he's going to come back, announce to me that he's getting married.' 'Be patient, darling,' Eugène said vaguely. 'Be patient? You idiot! Wait until autumn? He's just arrived, it's spring. Ah, your spring is beautiful! Two degrees above zero at seven in the evening. Watch your grapevines!'

César's window was so frost-covered that he could barely make out the motionless, menacing lake; towards seven o'clock, the water looked less smooth, was pricked with needle points, it was raining, sparsely, the drops held up in the clouds by the frost. 'Just enough to wet the vineyard, and if the weather clears up towards morning . . . ' At ten, the thermometer placed next to the parlour windowpane showed zero Celsius. 'Are you listening, Eugène? You aren't going to bother me all night long, nor budge from here.' Lying on her catafalque-bed, she was hastily cleaning her fingernails. Eugène heard César pacing in his room, opening the door, coming down the stairs. Two below, three below zero. Everywhere in the village, houses had their lights on, half-naked men were peering into the night, feebly lifting their hands, the fishermen were thinking about their nets which, if tossed up towards the sky . . . But more fleeting than the fish-filled waters, the clouds were slipping off to the west, a few stars could already be spotted. 'The rain, and now these clear skies.' César was coming down once again, his dangling braces striking his red-haired legs. The veiled moon, turning pale and clear like the face of a dead woman, was shining into the stairway with its molasse-stone steps. Now he was going back up, sitting down next to the window; this is how he saw the dawn whitening the sky, then between two glaciers the criminal appearing—the red sun. The men came out of their houses, ran towards the vine-yards and crushed the shrivelled black sprouts between their hands. While Madame, who was having her breakfast—Their vineyards! Their stupid vineyards! They deserve it—started speaking about hygiene and architecture. She was surprised *in petto* that people who knew her were not imitating her, that every woman within thirty miles did not resemble a statue erected in the middle of a town square, with a man wearing a Chinese hat playing music at her feet, she was sur-prised that her lifestyle was not adopted, imitated, by compatriots to whom such a model was put forward. It must be said that she had decided to live incognito; in her completely personal way, she contented herself with bending her earth-sized head over Isabelle's suitors, the man from the canton of Uri, Dogodela, Pepin, the gentleman farmer, with responding to the animals that loved her so, the gulls soaring above the blue gardens in front of the windows, the swans trundling along behind her on the shore, Bella in the stable. As to girls of marriageable age, they came rushing out from everywhere, like a forest fire that Madame was trying to stamp out with her big bunion-bumpy foot.

'Fortunately I put things in order, back then, after that wedding with Blanche . . . '

'You?' he dared to object. 'You? You mean Providence?'

'Call it whatever you wish . . . And why isn't César, if I may ask, going to act as a guide at the glass factory as had been arranged?'

Waiting in vain for him in front of the glassworks is an impassive Lady S., her shopping bag full of Oberland chalets; the director is wringing his hands: 'Haven't you seen him? Where could he be? A handsome man? With red hair?' César takes the liberty of going out in the evening without saying where he's going.

Set down within the night, the village feast, smelling of spruce and acetylene, was spinning like a world. It was far from here, in the Lowlands, at the edge of another lake. A six-foot-long catfish was swimming along the shore and, seeing the lights from afar: 'Let's hurry up,' it whispered, 'I'm going to arrive too late.' But a fisherman brought it back in his nets and the next day he stood it up straight on its tail and had himself photographed next to it. The horses from Mélanie's area were galloping over the plateau dominating the Lowlands and, coming to a halt, they rested their long wooden heads on the boulders and gazed at the lit-up carousels. César was arriving from Fraidaigue and, since it would have been impossible to get all the way over there in one evening, he rose at times into the air and pedalled above the fields. Where are the children? he was musing. Between them and us . . . He sat down at a table, a young girl soon slipped between the wall and the bench, ordered a lemonade, she had bright brown eyes, a pink silk blouse moist at the armpits, César paid for the lemonade. 'If you wish,' she said. They danced, she was a servant at the mayor's, she would step back, step forward in her fine Sunday shoes. The brass band stopped playing; the immense crowd standing around the feast was afraid of this big bonfire in the countryside, the owls were perched in twos on the branches, all feathers and silence, and there were those insects whose thin cadavers are all that can ever be seen on Gwen's windowsill, next to the pink and blue pebbles brought by César at dawn. 'Where do you come from,' the girl was asking César, 'you're not from here. Do you have a long road ahead of you?' 'Oh, I can quickly get up on high,' he replied vaguely. And he offered her a nougat, a paper rose won at a shooting match, then he left the circle around the bonfire. The road followed a lake where, some twenty-five feet below the surface of the water, a giant catfish was swimming, and then the road climbed away from the Lowlands, towards cherry-tree country. Alphonsine would go out on Sunday evenings, César would fly most of the way to catch up with her, the men up in the cherry trees, pulling apart the branches whose leaves are making storm-like noises, would watch him fly by. In the undergrowth, the sand shows through, the willows are grey and green. And if he found the children on that very beach! Between them and the adults whom they had become—Eugène beneath Madame's bunion-embossed slipper, the hypocritical Adolphe, Zoé crazy or pretending to be so, and he, César, having taken refuge in the depths of a dark hovel—there is no longer any resemblance. Yet the children aren't dead, one would have known so otherwise; so they're somewhere. Then he would catch up with Alphonsine, following her into her modest room concealed by the turret of the outer staircase down which Monsieur de Saint-Ange would come back then, wearing his nankeen trousers and straw top hat. The woodpile is just outside, the room smells of wet wood and is full of earwigs. 'Here you are at last,' she would say, tall and strong, her nostrils buttery, as she looked him over. From his pocket he would draw some red-current candies with a white cross, placing them on the bedside table, she would struggle to close the shutters of the window covered with bars. The shadows, the silence, so many more insects than people, were surrounding the village with its thirteen bonfires. 'But where do you live? Do you have a long way to go?' she was still asking. 'Me? Oh no, I can quickly get up on high.' She would drape his tight black overcoat around him, was he perhaps a solicitor? He would leave, sometimes flying over the fields, without doing so he wouldn't be able to reach Fraidaigue before dawn. He was thinking about the Isle of Contraries formerly inhabited by the children, peopled with six eleven-year-old brothers, with Eugène imagining himself marrying his mother later on; then he chuckled to himself, for Alphonsine had just told him that she was expecting a child. When he came in sight of Fraidaigue, Madame was sleeping, Ulysse in his green room was frenetically measuring his dwarfed arm. 'I'll tell them . . . tomorrow.' The next day, Madame walked over to the stable on her big bunion-embossed feet, her head capped with those snowy staircases that wouldn't melt in the April sun; the bees were rubbing their legs and flying off heavily and distractedly. 'I've come to see Bella. Look! She recognizes me.' Startled, Bella moved backwards, making a big noise of hooves and floorboards. 'She wants to say hello to me. Oh, animals love me, the other day some swans were following me around. And, hey, have you seen that big bird often soaring around the tower? . . . But where were you yesterday evening, César?'

'I think I have the right to go where I please. At my age,' he added bitterly.

He turned his back on her, she was staring intently at the felt round to which his red hair was sewn.

'Where were you yesterday evening, César?'

Trembling all over, Eugène was rocking back and forth on his heels at the tower door.

'Where were you yesterday evening?'

He was lifting dung with his pitchfork.

'And all those other evenings? We were searching for you down at the lake. But the *Danaé* was there, pulled over to the shore. Where were you?'

In his tiny old bailiff's coat with its velvet collar!

He mumbled something incomprehensible.

'First of all, it's the servant's job to carry out the dung and manure. Why do you always stay here in the stable instead of coming to see us in the château?'

After so many years, his mouth started watering. So it wasn't a château where she had formerly lived, with medicine, hygiene, architecture playing at her feet? 'I know all that,' she would often mumble. 'All that is known,' she would add even more mysteriously while recalling that grand creature riding in a too-small fiacre one foggy evening. A father was walking next to her and holding the hand, enclosed in a white leather glove, that she held out to him. The unfortunate marriage proposal had barely been made the next day by Eugène when her parents died, her father who wore a flowing beard and would lean his elbows on the false terracotta urn full of leaves and slugs that adorned their small garden, her mother who secretly feared the servants who could still be encaged in rooms which had barred-over windows and to which, in the evening, they would bring back a chunk of bread that they set on a box between their psalter and their steel watch. The father and the mother died immediately after Eugène's marriage, the former of a stroke, the latter of appendicitis, the doctor arriving too late, drawing from his fob the turnip watch of the 1883 Federal Shooting Match that he had inherited, along with a polar-bear hide, from his father the gold digger. The only witnesses of Madame's childhood were dead.

'Where were you yesterday evening?' she asked again. 'Aren't you happy with us? Apparently not, for you're always in the stable or lying on the sand. It's a bad example for the children, I say.'

'And,' he said, 'if I left?'

'To the Maison d'En Haut? You've just arrived here.'

'No, elsewhere, I don't know where . . . But my own place.'

'Really? But live where?'

Indeed, where? Fraidaigue? The Maison d'En Haut? But what about Eugène then, and Adolphe?

'My own place,' he repeated softly, as if he were alone. 'And have children.'

'Have children? You, César?'

Madame looked him over closely. Then signs showed she was going to laugh. She indeed laughed, the windowpanes of the stable trembling although it had been solidly built by Armand, the father of Armand the builder; Rim and Rime came out of the pigsty, shading their eyes with their soiled hands, a window-pane fell out at the messenger's, she shuddered, lying riveted to her bed and wearing her beautiful green dress. César lifted his pitchfork, shoved it right through Semiramis who immediately stopped laughing and took on an startled look that stayed on her face, her walled-up-woman's big, lividly white hands stupidly dangling while he carried her, in his outstretched arms, to the manure pile. How heavy she was, those ankle boots full of stones! 'You see,' she was announcing triumphantly in the evening while taking off her boots in the bedroom, 'you see, he no longer goes out in the evening.' Alphonsine waited in vain on the shore of the other lake. I've said nothing to Alphonsine, César was thinking, at the back of the stable, she'll never find me, whenever she asked me if I were coming from far away I'd only answer: 'Oh, I can quickly get up on high . . . '

Order had been restored, but these alerts will kill me, Madame was saying, I who have such frail health and remain on my feet only out of sheer willpower. Sitting very straight on the settee, she was pretending to fall asleep, gently rocking back and forth, her eyes closed, to the great chagrin of the measly reading group that she was hosting that evening. The three friends, the Bytadez, had to pack up and leave. They tiptoed out, unknowingly walking over the site of the tower, the superimposed faces of the servants watching them from the barred-over window from which they couldn't spot the lake, only sometimes during windstorms would a few bits of foam flutter up in front of the bars. Dez was brandishing his tiny umbrella against a big fly that had escaped the autumn downpours and winter snows because it had found its Ark on a hornbeam leaf; Madame then emerged from her feigned sleep and thought amusedly about the Bytadez, about those three earthworms who would read Racine or Mme de Sévigné with her once a week and sometimes dare to allude to their own health! That By, for example, born in the countryside, whose aunt was burnt by the explosion of a spirit-of-wine lamp and who kept her right arm tightly pressed against her chest and was the first to stand up furtively to make the coffee. But when her sister was afflicted with rheumatism and also became crippled, the disabled woman put on some weight and blossomed in front of everyone's eyes.

'What are you doing there behind me?' the paralysed woman was stammering.

'Nothing,' she was replying, her little arm shaking out her sister's dress that she had just taken off a peg in the wardrobe.

'Go ahead, put it on,' the brother-in-law was saying, 'she'll be wearing only nightdresses from now on.'

He was thrusting the dress into her arms, she was going up to her bedroom, climbing up on a chair to see herself in the mirror. With a lump in her throat, the child was looking at her mother, a trickle of saliva dribbling from her mouth . . . As for Ta, he was writing books—fancy that!—and was mourning his son who, tipping his boater to the crowd, had gone up in a balloon and, blown out over the Atlantic, was never seen again. Madame sighed with boredom and cleaned her fingernails with renewed vigour. Isabelle . . . The night was completely black, a suitor was knocking in vain on the tower door. His elbows leaning on the balcony parapet, César was wondering if he would be able to spot the children on the lake with a good spyglass. The sun had left but a red glimmer in the west, seemingly the glimmer of dawn, the Earth was going to stop, start spinning in the opposite direction, everyone would change, Eugène would not marry Madame. With the Bytadez gone, she went out onto the balcony that was receding against the background of waves. Just as soon, César slipped outside to take a tour into the stable where the fire at the heart of the property burns, its crackling straw, its dark sparks and, like the soft burbling of a source amid burning wood, the dripping of black liquid manure. From afar he saw the servant lad breathing easy, for a moment, leaning against the stone doorframe, in the still air of an evening of reprieve. Isabelle was hesitating to finish the last square of needlepoint, Pepin the Short was leading his yellow-bonneted mother down the streets of Rouen, the man from the canton of Uri was piling up toothpaste tubes and toothbrushes in a flat, one of whose windows always remained shut. Of the marriageable men left for

Isabelle, the gentleman farmer and Jedermann's wretch of a son remained. The gentleman farmer, who during long winter evenings would leaf through an old Vermot almanac while whipping his boots with his riding crop, was in fact coming forward, scarred stiff, over the gravel of the terrace. He passed in front of the gazebo, with its sheet-metal pelmets, where the children would see the turtledove sitting and embroidering. Standing at the tower window, Madame was exploring the horizon, a big bird suddenly let itself drop onto the waters. The cannons of Alsace had chased the gentleman farmer's parents towards the south, they hastily left behind their Germanic march, filled up a train carriage with their whole family, the babies whose heads wound with padded cloth kept drooping because of the lead they have in them, and the maids wearing big butcher's aprons who kept righting them, the gardener became deaf as soon as he got out, they saw a beautiful pale-green house with an Empire-style pediment on the lakeshore, a rose garden, and a small port. *'Let's buy it,'* said the father, who had rings below his eyes and kept a dancer for a mistress. His wife was struggling to hoist herself out of the motorboat while the Prince of Gontaut-Biron, who had arrived to pay them a visit, was standing there on the tiny landing stage, sucking the golden knob of his walking stick; he held out his hand to her, though she was, it was said, merely a Basel dairyman's daughter who had been wed, '*let's do it,*' with a sigh of resignation, because she was pregnant. 'So, gentlemen, bon appétit!' she shouted joyously, clapping her hands to summon the guests to the table. Strawberries and cream. '*Oh, it's a treat,*' mumbled the Prince of Gontaut-Biron who was longing for his walking stick, with its golden knob, which he had placed, taking a thousand precautions, in an angle of the antechamber and which was now being ridden by one of the children with the padded diadem. But what's the Prince up to? He's asking for the salt. But, Prince, we're having desert! That's the point! . . . This is why the eldest son of the man from Basel, the gentleman farmer, ate, when he was Madame's guest, his apple with salt. Isabelle loved him as soon as she saw him walking over the gravel of the terrace, yet caught a glimpse too late of his bad teeth when he started to suck the golden knob of his walking stick. 'My brother-in-law, the brother of my husband'—Madame nodded towards Eugène—'owns, through his wife, large horse-breeding farms. They hunt in the autumn.' 'Truly, Madame,' said Jämes, annoyed, as he was groping between his knees for a crumb of a petit-four cake, the kind that the green-clad messenger goes to buy in the next town along this stifling lake. 'Gold-headed needles, messenger,' they would cry out to her, 'sweets, aniseed biscuits for tea,' and they would make the sign of four by raising their hands with the little finger tucked back against the palm; her handkerchief could be seen sticking out of the thousand folds of her green dress and, thanks to that handkerchief, at night—the mute earth was transforming itself into the moon, some kind of deaf fire was burning on the horizon— Armand who was leaning out of the tower window saw her coming and going, carrying away the swaddling clothes and the baptism robe of the dead child. The gentleman farmer, Madame's guest, ate his apple with salt. Madame took the saltcellar and delicately, with her little finger raised, also put some salt on her plate. Oh, we always ate them like this and if I haven't thought of it until now, it's because I live among these peasants. And she once again set the stare of her regal eyes, for hours, wherever he was, upon unhappy Eugène, who was visibly losing weight. After eating his apple with salt, the gentleman farmer quickly wiped his tawny moustache.

'But your field,' he said, 'that triangular field that separates us from the lake, near Les Guerres. I'd buy it at a good price, *a substantial price.*'

'This is a pretext,' thought Isabelle. 'He'd like to marry me. When a man speaks to you about his fields . . . '

'Money is a curse. Oh, it's a curse!' Madame abruptly asserted while rubbing the rust on her knitting needle into her greasy chignon. Abraham left the gazebo, where they were having coffee, went back up into the tower and neared the window, he was hardly thicker than one of the those big butterflies which, on summer afternoons, alight upon a flowered curtain, their paper-thin wings quivering in the shade of the bedroom sheltered by the château walls. César, who had taken refuge in the stable, raised his eyes and, spotting his nephew leaning out, sneaked behind the bushes, crossed the garden and slipped into the tower. The gentleman farmer went on to explain to them, apropos of the Duke of Guise who was living on the other side of the lake, that one must never say 'Guise' but 'Gu-ïse.' Then he pulled out his pocket watch and, mumbling *'Time is money,'* walked away across the gravel of the terrace.

'César!' shouted Madame angrily. 'César who has once again gone away while we were chatting so pleasantly. (At last a visitor worthy of me!) God knows where he is!'

César . . . César! God knows what he did all summer long, at times lying on the beach—do I myself have the time to lie on the beach?—at other times taunting her by going out at night without saying anything.

But it's Monsieur Eugène who sprawls out between the casks, getting himself showered with praise by the grape-pickers because he gives them two litres per capita for their labours instead of the one litre granted by the other owners, while, in the meantime . . .

'But, darling . . .'

'Shut up. You know nothing about your brother. Where does he go in the evening when he leaves the terrace where we are all sitting together?'

When he leaves the terrace after having closed the stable where the horse is trampling the straw and waiting for oats. He swings open the gate and heads into the street, the ancient waves have shaped the walls of the houses in their own image, and he looks aside so as not to see a clump of maidenhair fern.

'Am I my brother's keeper?' Eugène rashly retorts while cleaning his fingernails with a pocketknife; a golden chain bars his white waistcoat.

'Where is he?' whispers Semiramis, sitting in her gazebo. She thinks she's whispering, but they can hear her all the way into the tower, and all the way into the clock tower, all the way to the limit of the unseparated lands where the beings of the third day are standing behind the fishnets.

'Do you think he's at the engineer's? Or at Thomas the civil servant's? Or at the wine merchant's? Those fellows all have daughters.'

'But, upon my word,' says Eugène, 'then he'll have to be given his share.'

'His share? As if he hasn't gobbled it up ever since he has been eating at our table and sleeping in our sheets!'

'I'm going to ask the Rims if they've seen him.'

'But of course, darling.'

The penniless cousin was standing in front of his little realm, the old pig stable. When he turned his back on you and put his fist on his hip, meditating on his inventions and thinking with despair 'Oh, why don't we have the Lépine Invention Contest here?', his red moustache could be seen sticking out from each side of his head. Poor Rim! One day he had the idea to transport on lorries the lake water to the soldiers in the trenches, he bought a big plot of land to the north of the village, would he marry Isabelle? And he used the three war years to get the little round-headed cabinet maker to make a big secretary desk inlayed with gold and ivory. The cabinet maker abandoned all his customers, worked for three years on the desk, brought it to the villa in separate parts and put it together on the spot, but he had barely finished when a bailiff was seen coming up the central walkway, sponging off his forehead and kicking down the little beech trees, the little poplars. 'It's over,' he said, 'the war is over, you have to take away your jars, your buckets.' Rim would borrow even the lake vases that the fishermen dragged back in their nets and carried to the château, even if only one tower remained, the other one had been completely demolished by Armand the night after the turtledove died. For Rim, anything could be used, he took from the March sower the Lenzbourg jam bucket from which he would toss out his seeds, gathered up the rowboat bailing buckets, and even, towards the end, perched upon a lorry his own stoneware bathtub which he had in fact never had the time to instal and in which Édith would place her geraniums in winter—their pungent fragrance, those hairy leaves that the turtledove picked off to stop the bleeding whenever we had cut ourselves by whistling into a sharp blade of grass. The biggest problem was removing from the villa the gold-and-ivory-incrusted desk, an axe had to be found, the desk was taken out piece by piece, then abandoned in the hedge, Rim went away weeping over his property built on water, back then he would sail off on a big boat with russet sails, the children gliding by, through the morning haze, in their fishing boat. 'César!' the good Rim called out just as soon, for he knew that César had long been looking for the children. Never again will Rim's big boat be seen, now motionless, its sails brailed, breathing in the pure, deep lake water, like a butterfly, while the wind tries, no longer tries, seems to give up, finally tears it away from the rose it is clutching. One of poor Rim's tears falls on the vineyard at the very spot where the glass factory was later born. It was just after the Armistice, henceforth the soldiers would drink water from their fountains or their taps. In her tower, Madame, looking out for the doubtful arrival of the embassy attaché, saw cousin Rim coming forward, burdened with souvenir-recipients and wearing, pinned to his chest, the little gold bucket given to him by Lyautey during a banquet. Fraidaigue possesses, if one counts the tiny windowless room on the second floor—whose walls bear the pencilled names of the children shut up inside after the turtle-dove's death—fifteen rooms in all. Poor relatives can be put up on the back, garden, side. 'Édith, your shoes need resoling,' Madame immediately stated. 'At the little cobbler's at the base of the town clock. How can you go out with worn-down heels? As for me . . . ' She lifted her black skirt, showing—who would believe it?—that beneath its stone dress a city has two massive black leather shoes, chapped to look realer. Édith who had to give to the cobbler the two francs she had saved in her pitiful purse, turned her head away when she walked by the pastry-maker's shop window; she was wearing a wig, speaking in a low muffled voice, a black cotton thread sewn into her blouse. 'Your heels! Édith, what an example you are for the servants! For the villagers!' Édith couldn't even buy stamps to send letters to her beloved sister in America. Rim pinned the little gold bucket given to him by Lyautey above the fireplace with its stucco designs. 'You're fortunate to have a fireplace. Does some smoke blow back into the room? Leave the door open. And this view of the vegetable garden! What a pity that I will soon need to take this room back from you. You know, when my brother-in-law César comes back in the spring . . . Apropos of that, Édith, I'd like you to get rid of your habit of reading in bed in the evening . . . No, no, don't come down to the parlour when I have company, it's unnecessary for you to come down.'

'You go first, Édith,' she would politely order whenever they came across each other at the garden gate, and all the way up the staircase Édith would feel the unbearable stare focused on her heels as she climbed the molasse-stone steps that had been hollowed down by ancient footsteps and stained by the young dead woman's blood. 'I don't understand,' Madame would say slowly, 'how one can *live* with worn-down heels.' Rim would go up behind them, meditative beneath his big wine-grower's hat, ruminating about the countless little inventions constantly born in his brain. A filing cabinet, for example, in which files could be hung up simply by sticking them into a vast rubber sponge. But no one was interested in this invention, not even cousin Thomas, who put on his lustre oversleeves every morning. Ah, if we only had the Lépine Invention Contest here!

'How sad I am,' Madame was in fact saying, 'to take this room back from you. It's because my brother-in-law, César, is going to arrive from the Maison d'En Haut. Oh, it's not his room, naturally, but with that human being in the house . . . Oh that César, he's my cross. Perhaps you think that everything is rosy for me because I have a château.' She laughed unwittingly, showing her deep-sea-diver teeth. She would laugh two or three times a year, on an equinox day, on a solstice day, the windowpanes would tremble in the village, the messenger's windowpanes would fall out and down to the road alongside the houses tilted because of ancient waves, and Gwen would get up, barefoot, a golden curl on her shoulder, and grope for the lakeshore flowers that César had placed on her windowsill. 'But,' she would continue, 'come and see this pigsty—it's beautiful, at least in my opinion.' Armand, the father of Armand, the builder, had done his job well, solidly building both the henhouse and the pigpen. They would have a little stove whose pipe simply went through the wall, a rather muddy place in which to stay during nice weather. 'Ah, you're fortunate. It's a real little realm. And then you'll be so much better off here, so much freer than in the château.' At this word, she sneezed, the last remaining window-panes at the neighbours' houses shattered, the glazier, attracted by the noise, hurried out from town, running into the messenger, along the lakeshore, who was heading in the opposite direction and the wine-growers in the vineyards weren't seeing her coming back any more than they were able to see the coming of night or winter. The glazier set his transparent burden down at the foot of the willows, at the spot where Rim's desk was very slowly returning to its tree state. Poor Édith would detour whenever she went to the vegetable garden to gather some herbs for the soup, but in vain, because she was forced to walk past the gazebo, raised above ground level, where Semiramis' walled-up-woman's big, lividly white hands were hanging straight down at her sides. She would mumble, 'Your heels, Édith!' Fortunately, Édith's mother was dead; her father, too, in fact, for he had himself fallen while holding ropes for acrobats. Next to Semiramis' gazebo was the entrance to the room where the summer toys were kept, at the back there was a stone stage with a ceiling so low that the children couldn't stand up unless they bent their pigeon-like necks, but Zoé the Queen was lucky, she was seated on the only chair, a folding stool with a green velvet seat.

'Where's César? Have you seen him? Just a while ago he was with us in the gazebo. Oh, you were right to stay down here, it's *unnecessary* for you to come when I have company.'

César had furtively gone up into the tower and was standing behind Abraham, who was leaning out of the window. 'What are you doing, Abraham? You're leaning out too far, be careful.' As the wind blew over the two vast meadows of red tiles structured by the rooftop, it was making a clump of maidenhair fern quiver. 'Be careful, Abraham, an inch farther and you'll fall down to the beach. It's said that one faints before hitting the ground.' Abraham hears César breathing heavily behind him and Semiramis whispering: 'At the civil servant's, at the evangelist's? . . . ' From up there they can see the hairstyle that she re-creates every morning by jabbing needles thick like pitchforks into her hair. Édith comes out of her stable and, despite her mud-covered heels, Madame cries out, 'Édith, how you walk!' She lifts her skirts, imitates a duck waddling along, the swans at the edge of the water raise their heads and, beating their big clumsy wings, lose a few feathers before trundling off down the shore. For Abraham and César, who are still leaning out the window, not only Édith's worn-down heels but all of Édith seem to sink into the soft soil, the dogs all become basset hounds, the pigeons and the hens are flattened out against the ground by the columns of air joining them to the sky and vibrating in front of the tower windows, which lack panes. 'Where's César? Have you seen him? I'm always worried when he goes out in the evening, he's such a child, a girl could wheedle him.'

A squirrel scurried down the sycamore, Rim raised his eyes and spotted, at the tower window, some red hair behind Abraham's shoulder.

'Your mother,' the red hair was whispering, 'oh, she says nothing, but you'll never go to foreign countries and learn to play the flute. Ulysse! Poor Ulysse! Barely good enough to count grape-picker's baskets. And for all the litres that have come out of the harvest these past years ... It's you, Abram, who'll take over the property. From morning to nightfall, the vineyard, the chores, the hail, the frost, the coulure. Ah, everything was different when we were small. And you can believe me, Abram, we'd walk on this fine roof to gather moss and maidenhair fern. Lean out, Abram, lean out and look at Isabelle's suitor walking away down the beach.' The gentleman farmer seemed snapped up by the sand. He placed one foot here, one foot there, and murmured, '*My God, I shall not die.*'

'But where's César? Answer me!'

Then, without knowing why—in order to put himself in a favourable position with respect to Madame? (But that was absolutely useless)—Rim motioned with his chin, as that nasty little traitor Mateo Falcone had once done, at Abraham and César at the tower window.

'You see!' she immediately shouted at Eugène, who came closer, trembling. 'You see, he wasn't at the evangelist's or at the civil servant's at all. What foolishness! I'm always right. He was in the tower with Abraham, that's where he was. It's because he loves his nephew so much. Oh, he adores his nephews, that you have to grant him.'

She pointed up at them with her walled-up-woman's heavy hand, then spit into the gravel and, recalling hygiene, crushed the spittle under her bunion-bumpy foot. What a doctor she would have been! Leaving the Rims there, she headed towards the château. 'That César, what a cross! Just a while ago, he was in the tower, but then, but then! Ah, if I had been told way back when . . . ' When a fiacre entered the fog and an old man, who had no seat because of his daughter's dress, was walking along the snow-covered pavement. 'Shut up, Eugène, and realize once for all what would happen if he remarried! And if he claimed his share this time? What could it be taken from? We don't have a cent left. Nor does Aldophe. Yet it's Adolphe who doesn't have any children . . . Anyway, pay off the interest by taking out a mortgage? On what? And how can Isabelle be married off?' 'He'd have liked to marry me,' Isabelle would say in regard to the assistant director of the glass factory, 'I'm the one who didn't want to.' In the environs, the grapevines were getting scorched by that false church blazing night and day. 'But why wouldn't he find a job at that glass factory? Oh, I don't mean blowing glass but guiding visitors around. That's what I'd myself like to do!'

'Does he go off to see women?' the servants were wondering, their faces superimposed behind the window, pierced in the wall tilted by the ancient waves, and they were watching out for César, who would be going by, after Rim's denunciation had forced him to come down from the tower. Sitting in the middle of the stable courtyard, Rim in fact regretted his act; seeing Abraham thrown down to the base of the tower by that bastard César would have somewhat embellished their, alas, quite boring lives. Night was falling; the column of air placed upon the head of every human being, of every pigeon, was turning vaguely phosphorescent, the village had its luminous counterpart in the sky. Did César go off to see women? So the servants were wondering. Elsy, perhaps? Elsy wore polished high heels and a black silk dress stained brown under the arms. 'Where's César going? Where's your brother going?' Madame was asking while stamping her heavy stone feet. 'Am I my brother's keeper?' But suddenly Eugène shuddered: Madame was staring at his neck; this had been her habit for some time now, and try to go about your work, manage this half-solvent property, watch over the fishnets, give orders to the wine-grower, with that dart in your neck! The waves beating against the shore observed from afar those tilted walls and had not forgotten their saltpetre taste. César entered the cabaret, Elsy was traipsing over to the tables, the out-stretched hands of the drinkers trying to grab her, she escaping from them, flying through the hoops, some-times losing a shoe or posing for a second on a table, her rounded bosom brushing against purplish ears, it was starting to get cold, a hare was already hanging in the courtyard, blood trickling from its mouth. The grapes are in, the lights of the inn are being reflected in the asphalt.

'But why, God in heaven, isn't he leaving for the Maison d'En Haut? The grape-picking is nearly over. For all that there was, besides!' 'Don't get him worked up, darling, I beg you.' 'It's true, this afternoon he was with Abraham, in his room. Oh, he adores my children, you have to grant him that. But how many times have I told you: "Go, go to the stable, he's been inside it all alone for days on end. God knows what he's thinking about.'"

Eugène was stretching his braces, his blue-veined feet inside the slippers that Isabelle had embroidered before Pepin's mother had taught her how to use filet lace.

'And you've forgotten, I bet, that next year is a leap year, the engineer is going to open the Pont des Machines, we'll see him coming around on his houseboat to inspect the beaches, and his daughter will be with him. Another girl!'

She lay down on her wheeled catafalque and hastily cleaned her fingernails.

'Or else he's at the cafe with that waitress, or at the fair with that woman at the shooting gallery. But be it this girl or that one, the civil servant's niece or the engineer's daughter . . . I beg you, shut up. We were lucky the first time, but it's not every day that a woman gets run over on her honeymoon. Oh, it's too much!' she suddenly shouted, her podgy arms, inside the narrow sleeves of her nightshirt with its scalloped lace wrists, waving in the air, 'My father told me so . . . '

He was walking next to the fiacre, ever-more distinct as one came closer to him, holding that hand, that white glove full of wet sand, that walled-up-woman's heavy hand.

'Do you know what you should do? You should get dressed again, leave for the fair, or the cafe, and bring him back. But that's not what's happening, Môssieu is taking his time brushing his teeth.'

If he hadn't already slipped into his nightshirt, how much he would have taken advantage of the furlough and run to the inn! He would have spoken about politics or history. Some people would even half stand up when he entered. The Monsieur from the château.

'Can you imagine us with that shooting-gallery woman in our family?'

She had swanlike eyes painted up each side of her head and would load the rifle, gazing from afar at the Ferris wheel drawing up human beings in its sand buckets, at the merry-go-round spinning like a little world from the past and sending up a faint column of light into the sky. César, who had replaced his mottled rope tie with a beige-and-white-striped cardboard one fastened with a rubber band, was aiming at a target and winning a rose that she pinned to his buttonhole while looking on with her swanlike eyes, the heavy rifle now placed against the rubble-stone wall made of cloth flapping in the northwest evening wind. César turned around and noticed the pugilists and face-slappers in front of Thomas' bride dressed in a black velvet cape and a long dress hiding her bunion-bumpy feet; her sewn hands were dangling at her sides. The soft violet velvet balls would hit the faces of the bride's aunt, the notary, Thomas the woodcutter, and Death, who would all fall backwards, their screams muffled, only their creator hearing their poor heads striking the strut holding up the cloth wall. One would have liked to know if the bride's arms were as heavy and cold as the one held out from the fiacre to the old man walking on the pavement. Alas, poor Thomas, César was thinking, if it had been she standing riveted to his side! No way to go to the inn, to spout off about politics with the villagers gathered around him. How had poor Thomas showed up at this stand? Because life is not simple for a little woodcutter who lives in a cabin far from the hamlet and meets up only with the pharmacist out hunting for mushrooms, his steel lorgnon attached to a tiny chain. César grasped the ball and hit the bride smack in her face, twice, thrice, ten times. She would fall backwards but spring right back up, standing there in her black velvet cape, creating a draft of cold air, and staring at César. Above the fair, a big clown with glittering skirts was flying around in circles. An hour later, César was watching him from his window. The next day Madame came down to breakfast while hastily cleaning her fingernails, her green dress concealing her feet and her sewn hands dangling at her sides. The fishermen had just brought back a Roman vase in their nets, but they hesitated to take it to a château with only one tower, and one of them suggested giving it to the museum curator who occupied a small shed built up against Fraidaigue; the village children would press their noses against the windowpane and watch him work, and he had been all shaken up and angry the day when Armand was throwing down stones from the top of the tower. Like Eugène, he wore a lorgnon and a celluloid collar, and like the engineer he had a daughter. All those daughters that these fathers had, and have no more! Actually, Madame is wrong to be afraid of those dead women. Eugénie, the curator's daughter, lived, when she was alive, in a little house near the glass factory, with a big blue cross standing at the entryway to the garden and a red-nosed dwarf squatting in the grass.

'Here's what will happen to you if you drink alcohol,' Eugénie says to the wine-grower who is dancing heavily in the winepress room, two dahlias stuck into his leather cap. 'Here's what happens when you go to the cafe,' she says to two children who have come to see the dwarf and would remain there for a long time holding hands if their mother, an apron over her head—it's raining on the abbey, the shooting gallery, poor Thomas' wedding party—did not come to fetch them. Eugénie is dusting off the life-size goose placed near the water spurting up from the fountain by the curator who had brought it back under his arm from Germany, after having exchanged it for a horse between Heidelberg and Stuttgart; now the horse leads the Junker to his factory through the morning fog, sparks flying from its hooves, the sand is yellow as if the sun were shining on it, the sails are sliding along the ground, Pepin the Short is embarking on the canal. Eugénie was surely not beautiful; Gwen . . .

'But look, César, I'm cleaning up my father's garden.'

'Eugénie . . . If I could obtain my share.'

'And what would you do, César?'

'I would live at Fraidaigue. It would indeed be their turn to live six months here, six months there, put up, fed, furnished with light and clean laundry. And to pay only their old-age insurance. Or else go and live in the stable.'

'But I thought . . . Madame said . . . Aren't you going to take on a little job at the glassworks? And why don't you rent one of those nice flats that they built for the glazers, beyond the train tracks?'

When Eugénie had finished dusting off the goose and turned around:

'César! César! Where are going off to?'

And what, César thought as he walked onto the beach, if I prefer lying on the sand to guiding through the glass factory those girl cousins from the Franche-Comté who have arrived like animals in their wooden compartments. The cousins could see from afar the top of the tower moving above the trees, shutting, opening, its white eyes. 'But I don't know, I assure you I don't know,' the director was saying, 'where could he be? Haven't you seen a handsome man with red hair? His sister-in-law, the lady from the château, had promised me that he would come today.' He was biting his fingernails while Lady S. was coldly awaiting her tour and gripping a big embroidered bag full of bears and chalets. Beneath the concave sky, convex for the dead, the Earth was spinning, the lake following it docilely and licking César's fingers reaching out to a spot between the ground and the water. 'If only,' Madame was thinking at the window, 'he could be dragged off by the waves, the engineer closing the Pont des Machines and the water flooding the beach while he was sleeping.' The engineer with his big head, black moustache and aquiline nose would finger the little key hanging on his watch chain between a star and a blue enamel crescent; he so much resembled Punchinello that he was very careful not to lean on the wall, someone might pull the string and he would remain riveted there, arms and legs extended. 'Come down,' his wife bristling with curlers would shout, 'come down right now, you idiot!'

The Pont des Machines had been constructed with the money of the lakeshore residents, some of César's savings and the piggy bank of Auntie Jean who kept her false teeth soaking in moon water and who died beneath her flowery cloth curtains from which were dangling garlands of the white-cotton cherries that she picked while she was dying. On the 15th of October, Punchinello opened the gate of the locks, vast waters came rushing through headlong, this was what the August lake full of lightning had been hiding, those big foamy beasts that carried off the light pink and blue pebbles which César, in the past, would place on Gwen's windowsill. Gwen's little face could be seen more clearly now, a golden curl flowering on her shoulder. The engineer had barely opened the locks when the lake became choppy in front of Fraidaigue, the children bobbing in their fishing boat, on the expanding beach appeared the Roman vase that the fishermen had brought back to the château, but for what use? Much time had gone by since the young dead woman had left him, walking over the white roses fallen from her coffin the evening before. Every leap year, the engineer arrives at Fraidaigue, pays a visit to the lakeshore residents, verifies the quays and the beaches, his poor Punchinello lower back enveloped with a cat hide from which paws dangle over his cold and coarse-grained derriere. He goes over and leans that poor lower back on the Fraidaigue wall where the maidenhair fern grows, where, every equinox, the Chinese hats and one-legged men stop and play music; then he hurries away: he had had a narrow escape, had himself been standing just below the tower window from which it would have been so easy for Madame to pull the string, she would have started guffawing with her cow's laugh, and then his wife might have shown up as well . . . No, Monsieur César wouldn't have my daughter Amélie. First of all, where would they live? At Fraidaigue? At the Maison d'En Haut? Off he went, shaking his head and muttering, keeping to the middle of the street because of the pulleys looming over it and hoisting up bundles of firewood. As usual, Madame was blocking the view through the one measly embrasure on the lake side; standing behind her, Eugène was rocking back and forth on his heels and tiptoes and stretching his neck to glimpse a sail. 'God knows what he's going to do this time, here's the engineer and his daughter. Do you remember what happened four years ago? Oh!' she suddenly shouted, 'I sense he's going to get married again. And I'm never wrong. There she is, arriving with her father in his houseboat.' A swell deposited on the beach a lake flower, a light pebble that would have to await the November storms to join its sisters once again since the beach was expanding little by little, Jedermann's son on the other side of the gulf was readying to come to Fraidaigue as he did every leap year. It's also from the beach that the wine merchant was arriving, on this last nice day of the year. César raised his head as he passed by. A belted, double-breasted black overcoat with a velvet collar. And the merchant's daughter? She's tall and beautiful. The year before, César had invited her to the village feast given for the abbey. 'But my God, let's finish once and for all with this marriage hanging over our heads! Let him marry this one or that one, I wash my hands of it. I'm fed up with retaining him in the parlour with my conversation, with going to see him in the stable—Bella loves my visits so much!—with turning fathers against him.' She was now going down to see the fathers, talk to them, stare at them, gesticulating with her walled-up-woman's big hands. 'I could have married the town doctor . . . Oh, what am I saying about a doctor? The mayor, the president! And now that good-for-nothing, that lazybones with his carrot-red hair, could throw us out? Of course he won't, how stupid I am (me, stupid?), he adores his nephews, he wouldn't want to see them out on the road.' The merchant sitting across from her, his big pale head borne by a too-small body clothed in black, was speaking of his daughter who was going to come back from boarding school, Madame was impatiently sighing and furiously cleaning her fingernails; he lived in town in a plain yellow house stuck down on a treeless square without a fence around it; the October winds would shake the house, carrying inside the smell of dead leaves, carrying back out the stench of the lavatories. As soon as he had set down on the table the first payment for the wine, he left as fast as he could, transfixed by Madame's weighty stare. He could barely squeeze his way into the street, the threatening houses coming ever closer, already striking the full casks. And what if, one summer, they united with the trees?! But summer doesn't last long enough in our climate. 'He's gone now, thank God, and this time he didn't bring his daughter.' He had paid for a small portion of the wine with gold coins. Standing on the balcony, Semiramis was pondering them in her strong white hands. Ulysse the Deformed was gardening. All of a sudden she started throwing the gold coins, one by one, into the vegetable garden. 'There you are,' she shouted, 'seven gold coins! Hey, Ulysse, pick them up! One in the rhubarb, one in the parsley, two next to the pink poppy.' Dragging his deformed leg along, Ulysse was struggling to pick them up. 'Hey, over there in the rhubarb!' But despite her globe-sized head, she couldn't remember where the seventh coin had fallen; it was never found. When the gentleman farmer had left, Isabelle tossed what remained of her filet lace patterns into the fireplace. Meanwhile, a new suitor was getting ready in a house looking out on a big garden extending all the way to the lake, a young theology student, his head bowed, cradling a too-heavy briefcase as if it were a lamb. The garden was resounding with the guests' laughter, the rich merchant was sitting at the table on the terrace next to his lovely young mistress, but the others saw only a woman with a red wig, her cheeks like orange peels. From the end of the garden, voices were shouting, 'Jedermann!' Those voices were the threatening trees leaning towards one another and speaking by shaking their leaves as they do in the summer which never lasted long enough to carry out their plots against human beings. The merchant dragged out his arm, draped in the midnight-blue cloth of all the shameful pleasures, motioned to the orchestra, six men wearing white jackets stood up together as if to piss, all the while giving full-teeth smiles; wretched Saint John was turning his head away. The Virginia creeper was already tossing out a frail arm towards the unmoving boy watching the well-lit table from afar and, above it, the column of fire joining it to the sky. He was at last fleeing over the exposed beach, the lakeshore residents had paid to construct the Pont des Machines, the winepresses would no longer be flooded every autumn, the children would no longer do acrobatics on the footbridges stretching from cask to the next, the girls for César, the suitors for Isabelle, would arrive at Fraidaigue by walking along the strip of half-watery half-solid ground left to their lot by the Creator. Haughtier than ever, Madame was eating her apples only with salt, she now needed vast quantities of salt for her daily consumption! The messenger was hurrying off to town; now that the harvest was over, the monumental doors through which the wine had been brought in were closed, César was once again leaving for the Maison d'En Haut, stopping at the corner from which could be seen a fragment of the vast meadows of tiles flowered with mosses and maidenhair ferns, trampled by his father's rubber overshoes when, in wind blowing his hair every which way, he crossed the roof to demolish the ruined tower from which the turtledove had fallen. Beyond the meadows of tiles, the grey lake rises to the base of the mountains, the light pink and blue pebbles are drifting in the depths, it's time for the metals to show on the surface, the lake to become iron-coloured. Farewell, grapevine, my queen of plants, farewell, bare earth in scrolls and shells, raised up, transfixed by air, phosphorus and lightning. Earth! Earth!

At the bottom of the avenue leading to the Maison d'En Haut, Mélanie was waiting for César; in her homeland there was also a lake, but it was green and pocket-shaped, underground streams flowed into it after having often vanished and reappeared once again. The horses galloping over the earth come to a halt, shiver and leap in a single bound over the invisible stream. Mélanie's mother had raised Lord Arthur until he left for secondary school with his vassal, the curate's son, on a mail coach burdened with trunks and a large-mouthed servant wearing tight, white-and-green pékin-silk leggings. Once through the gate, as she recounted years later to little Mélanie, the house was still two and a half miles away, a padded barouche with rubber tyres would take you along in dreamy silence, the hall was planted with marble columns . . . In short, the interlocutors were wondering, was an oak trunk burning in the fireplace? Of course! And behind the marble forest began a gigantic stairway, the brooms vanishing at dawn as soon as the servants had swept up while singing:

Hoi ho, hoi ho.

And on Sundays a clubfooted statesman would debark in a tilbury. Lady Basil would glide through the hallways and remain in the lavatory reading Shelley for hours, despite having taken Krüschen Salts Laxative for breakfast, and when she walked past the equestrian statue of Wellington on Sunday mornings in Saint Paul—the same statue which they wanted to erect in Pestalozzi's honour and to which ignorant people objected because they had not seen, like me,

Pestalozzi, the orphan of Stans, riding his dapple-grey horse through the sky alongside Plague and Famine on their black steeds—she would loudly exclaim to Lady Ann, '*Look, darling*, he's your cousin.' In the evening, Lady Ann would ask, 'May I dance in front of your guests, Mummy?'

Having glimpsed from afar Lady Ann dancing for Oscar Wilde—and then sleep in a twin bed next to the wood merchant! He would stretch and make his braces snap, sucking on his moustache beaded with fog, during those autumn days when the smothered heart of the Earth can be heard beating, when César is almost happy at Fraidaigue because he goes from the night of the morning to the night of the evening and can make out the children through the haze.

'Well, well, that's amusing . . . ,' the wood merchant was saying while sucking on his fog-beaded moustache. 'That young lieutenant, that Adolphe, as he's called . . . Well, he's asking me for our Mélanie's hand.' It seems that he's not even settled in his own family. 'Have you seen this photograph?' Photographed by the chiropodist-photographer, Adolphe was holding a book between his fingers, behind a table covered by a rug with pompons; his brother's wife was looking you over closely; her husband Eugène, their children Isabelle, Abraham and Ulysse, were carrying all the sins of the world on their shoulders. 'It's true he spoke to me about a second property that they supposedly own, higher up. All the same, Adolphe needs to be pretty bold to . . . Simply because he lived here during his military service . . . Ah, Mélanie, you've been here all along? I didn't hear you come in.'

It was dark in the larch-panelled room. Outside, it was already snowing, the woodcutters were pulling on the blocks and tackles to bring down the firmament, nothing could be seen ten steps ahead.

'But what's the matter, Papa, and who are you talking about?'

'About that young Adolphe who's dared to ask for your hand in marriage, you the daughter of a big-time wood merchant.'

'Really? Monsieur Adolphe?'

Mélanie's neck became marbled with red.

'But . . . What did you answer?'

'Nothing at all. Get a position, then come and ask for my daughter's hand, and you'll get a answer. Well, that's it.'

'But he told me that they have two properties, one of them a château with some vineyards along the lakeshore . . . ("Ha! A château!" silently sniggered her mother knitting near the window. "As if they knew what a château is!") . . . and the other the Maison d'En Haut as they call it, which has come down to them

103

from an uncle whose only son died by falling out of a walnut tree. A sister, he told me, lives with him. Oh, what did you answer?'

'How's that, Mélanie? You'd like to leave us, you our only child? All the same . . . If you have children,' he concluded bitterly.

She burst into tears. She wasn't pretty, her yellowish skin had red dots like a trout's, if only she had slipped away below the surface, what luck! But she was living in rooms, in the Jura, smelling of gentian and centaury. A revolving door with coloured glass panels prevents the air from penetrating the grey and blue paved hall, the sky trying in vain to enter from the other side through the narrow windows with their triple windowpanes, for they know down there that strange fish swim among the stars; on the table, a psalter, some knitting, dried herbs. 'Daughter of mine,' says her mother, who raised Lord Arthur and who dreams of the valet with his large frogmouth and of Lady Basil gliding off to the pinecone-scented lavatories where she spends hours reading Shelley, 'daughter of mine, if you want to be pretty, put pink lampshades on your lamps.' Poor Mélanie! She has a big flabby mouth from which words come out shapeless; overcome by a sentiment of helplessness, everyone rivets his eyes on that toiling mouth, the nose gets involved, the words come out of the nose and smell like ants. Her father's father called himself a grocer, then a merchant; his only son earned lots of money during the First World War by transporting things from one place to another. 'What else might I transport?' he kept wondering, pushing his bowler back on his head and wearing a navy-blue jacket over black trousers bumpy at the knees. The noise of the Verdun cannons reached him. From afar he watched Rim progressing across upended fields, carrying a load of fresh water to the soldiers, and back home in the Jura, he would place his psalter on the windowsill and meet up with his horse-merchant pals, their broad faces tinged by the wind of the plateaus that bloats their black smocks embroidered in white and bears them off from one farm to the next where they rap sharply with one finger on the windowpane; they drape their whip around their neck. As for him, he would slip a yellow raincoat picked up on the battle-field over his navy-blue jacket. Mélanie was moving her big flabby mouth while counting the points of her goose-grey embroidery work, on the black-marble Prussian fireplace mantel had been placed an araucaria which had a neck adorned with a pink ribbon and was hoarsely reporting that it had been present when giant reptiles were born. In the silent room, the two women were listening to a very faint sound of water that no one could explain, and they were looking out for the reaction of their guests—those officers watching over the Jura—to their nest of tables in gold. Dressed in green like a beetle, Adolphe, when he entered the room for the first time, did not immediately see where the windows were because of the piles of wood for burning and domestic use that had been heaped up against the house. It was a Sunday, the merchant's wife prepared the starched shirt in the morning, inserted the cuff and collar buttons, and placed a pair of jersey long johns alongside because it was colder than it seemed. They were nonetheless able to go out around four o'clock and sit beneath the wrought-iron gazebo. All around them were blooming roses, a bead of dew or fog gleaming on the thick petals of one of them. Mélanie was breathing noisily, a smell of sweat reached Adolphe's nostrils, especially whenever she fanned herself with her paper napkin; Adolphe turned his head away; the rose was rocking back and forth like a beautiful Jewish woman in her synagogue.

'What do you call it?'

'What do you mean?'

'This rose.'

'Madame Caroline Testu.'

You needed to have a bird for a mother, a turtle-dove for a mother, to entertain for a second the notion to marry Madame Caroline Testu instead of that flabby Mélanie who was standing up to fetch some biscuits, who collided with the door of the house over there, whose thighs must be streaked with blue bruises. Well-Well was keeping his moustache up beneath his nose with the help of his thick chapped lips; when Mélanie is gone, when she has married that yokel, will the noise of the water in the walls perhaps cease? Mélanie was coming back, blushing from afar, her feet got entangled in the false unicorn plant that had spread across the path, she turned around and gave it a nasty look. A bird flew across the sky, they took it for a swallow, would the swallows be flying away already? The winter would be harsh, woe to that last horse! Although putting his arm around Mélanie's waist is like hugging iron rods, she is an only daughter, every year a thousand tree trunks will come down the road from the Jura to the lake, carrying with them white larvae hidden in their reddish abodes and desperate woodpeckers striking the bark with their beaks. She will also have the red-gold watch chain and the chain bracelet bought in Paris during their trip. With his knobbed knees and his bowler pulled down over his eyes, the merchant of wood and time evaluated in a glance the forests of the Île-de-France.

'One hundred and twenty people disappear every month in Paris,' he was announcing with glee on that first evening, a starched napkin tucked into his waist-coat, reading the newspaper propped against the carafe and only vaguely noticing the upper part of the faces of his wife and Mélanie both silent and sad because there were so many other women more ele-gant than they were. If he had gone out alone in the evening instead of lying between the damp sheets of the hotel and winding black velvet ribbons around his legs, his only remedy against insomnia, while his wife was knitting a sock and Mélanie was trying on all her dresses in front of the wardrobe mirror and then desperately going to bed, the ruffians whose whis-tles could be heard—'Listen, listen!'—would have taken him for a bobby because of his moustache and thrown him into the Seine. 'Come, I want to buy you a bracelet,' he said the next day. She was lingering in front of the Printemps shop windows. That white neck striped with a black necklace! 'Trinkets!' They entered Cartier's, Monsieur Cartier himself decorated for some unknown reason; he was half-gold, his stomach, his teeth, the frame of his lorgnon, possessed hunting grounds in Chantilly and would go there with a silk pocket handkerchief folded six times inside each shoe to make him a bit taller. Taciturn bandits, the colour of walls, were lurking for them outside, virgins with gnawed noses were pretending to hold up the walls, genies were scurrying over golden balls. They arrived at the big circus of the place de la Concorde where automobiles, with numbers painted on behind, were driving around between rearing horses and seals spurting water to the sky. 'Oh this sky!' the false policeman was saying. 'Ye gods, look at this sky! Upon my word, why have I brought you to Paris!' When they took the train back home, their drab grey fellow travellers formed an indistinct heap of pale faces, chalky shoe soles, whitish hands and chequered caps beneath the big glass roof lit up by a dark gleam. 'Wait, I have my schedule and my guidebook, I can tell you exactly what altitude we are at. Well-Well, one hundred fifty feet, how's that? It's something else than our mountains.' A cow that had been lying down got up on its forefeet when the express train went by; something else needed to be done before the cow was completely standing, but what was it? The two genies glued to the train, their heads lowered between their outstretched arms, were rising and falling while singing like the spheres, like the Aeolian harp in the garden, the evening of the children's ball with its Venetian lanterns. 'Well, we've left the Île-de-France for about five minutes now. Look, the sky's no longer the same, one indeed says an Île-de-France sky.' They arrived home with black soot in their nostrils and a bracelet from Cartier's, Monsieur Cartier having himself been decorated for some unknown reason; their neighbour and rival, the horse merchant, saw them coming home, spotting them from the top of his tower that seemed to breathe in and out inside its stone corset. 'My hobby is architecture,' he would say while having his fake keep built in a way that made it grow larger towards the top. Birds attracted by the Satanic windowpanes would drop dead to the bottom of the tower as if it were the base of a lighthouse. The forest that began at a stone's throw from there continued all the way to the North Sea and was as impenetrable as a painted forest with its horses galloping in autumn over grass bent every which way by their hooves and the wind. The seam-stress hired to make Mélanie's trousseau was ringing the doorbell and thinking about her Gamba, about her Carlino, about how he would tap on his beret with a pole, the tiny house filling just as soon with white dust. Mélanie entered the parlour, exuberant in every way, how different she now was, how *prim and proud*, the gentleman farmer would have said, from Madame Caroline Testu. A smell of sweat would reach you, her pale eyes would turn tearful yet her tears were not salty, though no one knew this, she would collide with doors because of her tumultuous breasts and thighs streaked with blue bruises, and when she went out her feet would get entangled in the false unicorn plants growing across the roads. 'We'll see what happens,' murmured the merchant of wood and space, the false policeman, 'and if this noise of water in the walls ceases once Mélanie has gone. When she'll have married that yokel. All the same . . . ' He was undressing, his dangling braces sluggishly striking his amateur horseman's bowlegs. The next evening, while the deaf seamstress was biting a piece of thread to narrow it into a point and then raising both hands to hold it up to the window, while the departing day was dragging away all the light in its net, and while the birds were growing silent and listening to the soft sound of the net on the dead leaves, 'That boy, he no longer has his parents,' he suddenly said, 'I myself need to go to their Fraidaigue.' Mélanie brought her hand to her tumultuous breasts, where a little boat sometimes drifted. The next Sunday—'it's Sunday when farmers can be found at home, just walking around their lands, their hands behind their backs, looking around, rubbing the ears of wheat, tying up a grapevine shoot, those yokels!'—he slipped his black leather gloves onto his woodcutter's hands and, keeping his moustache up beneath his nose by grimacing, he trotted away on his horse. Around him, through the fog, the motionless horses seemed immense. His son would have been a dragoon, alas! He attached his mount to the cemetery gate, standing for a moment, redder than ever, his eyes burning with tears, in front of the unspeaking grave—however attentively insects lend their ears, not the slightest rustling of human elytra among the cypresses—where Gaston is sleeping in his little tartan shroud.

'Come on now, Adolphe's parents are no longer living, he's asking for Mélanie's hand, come on now, I have to go there.'

The countryside was moving along with him through the fog, the bushes suddenly budging and galloping off dreamingly here and there between almost invisible trees, coming to a halt, with shivering legs, in front of a moist fence. Attached to her territory, Madame Caroline Testu seemed worried as she watched him leave. On one of those evenings from the last summer when Adolphe came over to court Mélanie, he suddenly sniffed a fragrance of rose and said to himself, 'Actually, if instead of flabby Mélanie with those black rings around her eyes, her moist mouth—he hadn't yet learnt that her thighs were streaked with blue bruises—what if I married Madame Caroline Testu?' This is what it's like to have had a bird for a mother, a turtledove for a mother, a father who would demolish a tower so that he wouldn't see maidenhair fern any more. At Fraidaigue, César lying on the beach saw a stranger coming down from the train station. The sun was piercing the fog, distributing high noon from its hands of light to the small towns set in a crescent around the lake, the lightweight pink and grey pebbles, those lake flowers he would carry in the evening to Gwen's windowsill, were floating in the almost tepid water. He was vaguely daydreaming about a cheerful future; all in all, he was happy that Eugène, who had been the first child to marry, had taken Fraidaigue; he, César, would not have wished to have Fraidaigue because of the demolished tower from which the turtledove had fallen. The frightened children were listening to their father demolish the tower, then he set off in a boat, crossed back and forth all night long in front of the château and its painted windows, caught a bad cold and died. Not a single blade of grass grew where the tower had stood. He, César, would marry Gwen and take the Maison d'En Haut. But, then, what about Adolphe? Yet César had the right to it, he was the eldest child. But what would Adolphe do? Naturally, César was unaware of Adolphe's wedding plans and that it was a father heading down from the train station and taking the turn for the château: moreover, a mere trifle might have made it the father, not of Mélanie but, rather, of Madame Caroline Testu who was coming down to Fraidaigue to agree to Adolphe's marriage proposal; he would have doffed his boater just a little because of his half-bald head and greeted the woodcutters, the haymakers. It's not branches, leaves and hay that we are raking, they would then say to each other but, rather, roses! César was watching the sky darkening into twilight; a desperate red gleam was appearing in the east and reminding all God's children that the earth turns from west to east. A fine house that Gwen's parents had just at the corner of the promontory! A terrace looking out on the lake, a vast winepress room, 6,600-gallon vases, to the right the landing stage where three times a day the paddle boat churns forward, backs up, churns forward again, before finally docking. One day, Madame was sure to have spotted her embassy attaché on the first-class bridge, he was coming by land and water to the wedding of the young American woman and the King of Edom. The king's mother was resting in a big four-post bed with tiger hides piled on the sloping floor; a shelf made of boards and red cords was holding up as well as possible the collected works of Georges Ohnet. That day, among the diplomats being entertained was surely Madame's embassy attaché, a salamander was panting in the street gullied by the recent rains, a sky like a blue grape sprinkled with flowers extended above the little palace, it was five o'clock in the morning, the master of ceremonies was slipping on his dinner jacket, a valet was stepping over a bathtub pulled out on the balcony and carrying a cold suckling pig, the mother of the young queen, the tall American woman with dyed hair, at a window too small for her, was laughing in her terrifying way. Indeed it was he, our embassy attaché, in the middle of the procession, he whom Madame had met in a Venetian launch where she was squeezed in between him and a fringed black shawl, a glowing eye, a gold earring, and who confessed his ardent love to her on the isle of Torcello! Alas, the wedding procession vanished through the *trompe l'oeil* wrought-iron gate! One of the young women placed by the queen mother (who had come from Saxe-Coburg) between every soldier on duty on the towers—a soldier, a virgin, a soldier, a virgin . . . —suddenly had enough of these lethargic scarf games, fled all the way to the environs of Fraidaigue, ended up living with a painter who was Jedermann's neighbour, skinny-dipped, ate raw snails while shrieking out his delight and read poems to his cat. Lying on the beach, César, dreamily stirring his memories, was unaware both of why this stranger, who was coming down from the train station, was visiting and of the fact that, at that very moment, Fritz, who had just donned his corset, was leaving Bern for a two-day journey to ask for Gwen's hand in marriage, his exhausted horse stopping at the language limit, near that village over whose cherry trees fly angels who speak both languages and chatter loudly in the sky. Poor Gwen! If she leaves for Bern, the waters will definitively separate themselves from the lands, nothing more will be left for her except here and there, odd lakes spreading out between the pastures. Fritz had just spent six months in the Imperial Guard; Wilhelm II, over whose shoulders was draped the great white coat that Wotan had tenderly thrown to him to conceal his atrophied arm, would pass them in review next to his empress Frida wearing a tunic with Brandeburgs. On Gwen's windowsill were drying the gifts that César had been bringing to her since childhood, those light pebbles, those mosses with their tiny pink flowers. Set down like Fraidaigue on enormous slabs of stone, Gwen's mansion houses its inhabitants beginning on the first floor; the winepress room opens out onto the garden, on the side across from the beach, and the dirt floor on which flowers will grow only after thousands of years, slopes down towards the big vases in the same movement as the bottom of the lake whose waves, in stormy weather, beat against the walls.

'That César . . . ' says Gwen's father rolling breadcrumbs between his rheumatism-deformed fingers.

His wife sighs, 'How I would have preferred Fritz, who should be showing up from one minute to the next. In addition, he's a second cousin, Gwen would marry within the family. But what can be done? She has been attached to that boy ever since she was a little girl. May I presume he'll get the Maison d'En Haut? We passed by there the other day, do you remember? A lovely avenue and all that . . . In short, can we call it a family home?'

While she spoke, her tongue flapped like a stork; checking her chignon, she shrugged one of her shoulders, causing her right breast to jolt out of its corset stays, on which it fell back in an unsightly way. The lake was turning bottle-green, the waves foam-crested, the gulls were squealing the advent of autumn and their famine, Mélanie's father was ringing at the tower door, the one the children would open so easily with a dandelion stem. 'For Mummy,' they would whisper, 'for the turtledove, for the grey-feathered skirt.' The turtledove can now be made out more distinctly, she's short, wearing red leather shoes. Lying on the beach, his chin in his hands, a tiny shell, coloured like brown-and-white pekin cloth, dangling from the end of his red bangs, bits of rocks incrusted in his palms, César was dreamily watching a stranger who was sporting a bowler, struggling to keep his thick moustache up under his nose, and coming down from the train station; the baker's servant who'd swipe biscuits took a side street upon seeing the false policeman and slipped off behind the big fishnets that paint mist over the waters all year long. 'Is it true, is it true that Gwen's parents are awaiting me, as she told me yesterday?'

'Come on, is that César who's supposed to come really going to show up or not? *Is he coming?*'

He'd need to leave this sandy beach to which a bewitching spell keeps him chained, to stand up, to head left towards Gwen's house, to arrive at Fraidaigue and announce his marriage. The vast lake was breathing feebly, César digging his hands into the moist ground.

'Well, well,' the wood merchant was thinking with satisfaction, 'it's really a château.' That's what he was telling us in his green uniform, while I kept saying to myself: Long ways, long lies, like my mother-in-law who comes from the Baltic provinces . . .

He walked across the shadow of the demolished tower, the one that Armand destroyed during the nights following the turtledove's death, and this sacrilege will kill him beneath horses' hooves three years later. Well, well, so it's the sister-in-law. She looks like a city, sitting on the green velvet settee. (On which Madame Caroline Testu will be placed one evening when the inverted sky reddens in the east, when the terraqueous globe cracks and shivers like a lift that goes back in the other direction.)

'Well, well, I've just returned the visits paid to us by your brother, your brother-in-law,' he remarked, while hurriedly turning towards Semiramis, who contented herself with lowering her eyelids.

'Yes,' Eugène said politely, 'he had told them about that beautiful house in the Jura.'

'Oh, beautiful?! . . . It's you who have a beautiful mansion here, almost a château. Mine is big and convenient and not old. It's my father who built it.'

His father was a grocer who also sold bread loaves that he'd toss into the pans of a copper scales as big as a cradle, as well as surprise packets that were pink or purple wax-paper cones full of candies or with a ring so tight it could barely fit Madame Caroline Testu's finger whenever she hastily slipped on her little ankle boots over her green feet and showed up in the heights of the village: 'It doesn't smell of manure,' the valets of the stable would say, 'but of roses.'

'In short,' Well-Well was continuing, 'a business consisting of colonial foodstuffs, then of transport and of lumber. Here it's vineyards that you have? No fields? Your brother spoke to us of another château that you have higher up in the area, that you have inherited from an uncle, his only son having died by falling from a walnut tree?'

'Oh, not a château,' Madame said.

'Oh, a *small* château,' Eugène said.

Well-Well's forehead was creasing. Would this Maison d'En Haut, as Adolphe called it, have a tower larger at the top than at the bottom and squeezed into a corset like the one his rival had had built? His neighbour, his rival? They would mutually steal time and space from each other, the other one still wearing a farmer's black smock embroidered with white cross-stitches on the wrists, he had a big tinged face with a magnificent gizzard. The tower of his recent château-fort was adored with a sundial that bore a Latin motto that Joseph Dimanche, gone astray during the week, his whip around his neck, thought had been created for him. Standing at the tower window, he would look out on Mélanie's house, or else he would spray with lime the weeds in his garden, and the processions of ants would thereafter head for his neighbour's and climb the long wooden logs, Mélanie's dowry, which the woodcutters were beginning to load on wagons to take miles down towards the lake.

'Yes,' Madame keep repeating disdainfully, 'Adolphe told us that you have a very beautiful house.'

'Oh, beautiful, no, but not old, and large, well-heated, you know how it goes with these winters . . . '

'Well, my daughter likes your brother, your brother-in-law, she loves him, as one says, she knows how to keep house well, she spent two years with the cook, two years with the chambermaid, and boarding school, schools, and all that . . . Ha,' he suddenly exclaimed, 'everything would be fine if it weren't for that sound of water!'

He had summoned engineers, water diviners with their rods.

'Hey, well, it's like the sound of water that you hear coming from fires in a fireplace, but by Jove! We don't light fires inside the walls, or what?'

He was secretly hoping that the noise would cease with the departure of Mélanie, her tearful eyes, her moist mouth. Meanwhile, César, a tiny snail dangling from the end of his red bangs, was trying to get up, to extricate himself from this inexplicable weight: a fishnet had fallen over him. He managed to stand up, his shoes sinking into the wet sand, the irritated swans chasing after him as they used to do when he walked below the wall tilted because of ancient waves. He would only have had to turn left after leaving the beach and he would have gone beneath the windows of the messenger who, at that very moment, dressed in her green dress with its busk and bodice, was taking the stolen layette from the niche of the stove, because it was autumn and the time to heat would begin; and he would have arrived at Gwen's, before Fritz, who had donned his corset; she was waiting for him and had told her father he was coming. But despite the approaching sound of horses' hooves, he turned to the right and went back to Fraidaigue. 'Adolphe!' he heard called out cheerfully. Adolphe was cleaning his fingernails in his room full of mahogany furniture and draped with immense yellow-damask curtains. If the messenger had only stolen those instead of César's green curtains! Everything would perhaps have been changed. 'Adolphe!'

But Adolphe continued to clean his fingernails in front of his immense master-bathroom washbasin, behind him loomed the majestic bed on which Aunt Jean had died, on her bedside table a box full of used matches; in her death pangs, she ripped off the white-cotton cherries that fringed her Persian-fabric curtains. Aldophe kept cleaning his nails, if he had had eight fingers on each hand César would have arrived first—he was the eldest child after all, a fact that one tended to forget in this family—to say that Gwen was awaiting him, that he would marry her. But like everyone else, Adolphe had only five fingers, spatula-shaped, with furtively-bitten-down fingernails. A cheerful voice was calling out to him, he came down, saw César coming up the stairs, entered the parlour where Madame was sprawled out on the settee, where Mélanie's father was having a hard time keeping his moustache up between his mouth and his nose, and he placed his two enormous hands on his poplar walking stick; if you stick your ear to it, you can hear the sound of waves as you can in the giant prickly pink shell placed on the pedestal table in Mélanie's room.

'Ah, well, here's our man. In civilian clothes.'

Madame couldn't help but smile a little, revealing her deep-sea-diver teeth, and she raised her hands to the construction on her head, maintained by hairpins that the messenger, no longer than twenty years before, that August night when the turtledove stopped breathing—a veil of haze had fallen over the lake and the mountains appeared higher than the Gauri Sankar—went to town to bring back in the brown wicker cart. 'Hair curlers, a horsehair roller brush, a little flax fibre, cardboard, combs,' Semiramis had ordered. She saw César slowly raising his head and setting an unknowing gaze upon the four of them.

'Come on, Adolphe,' she said, nudging him.

'César, you're the eldest child. I want you to be the first . . .'

'Quick, quick, let me say that Gwen loves me, that I love her, that her parents will give me her hand.' But with his ears still full of the sound of the lake, he spent some time removing the snail dangling from his red bangs, and it was in a dream that he heard the end of the sentence: ' . . . the first to know that I'm getting married.' The false policeman, retaining his moustache by protruding his lips, made a ridiculous bow.

' . . . and that we're going to take the Maison d'en Haut.'

Of course. Where else would they go? Madame was genuinely smiling, the construction on her head, the dead town, was expanding throughout the entire room, it was becoming impossible to breathe, oh, how

I'd like to leave by the window, to walk along the stony path.

'And me?' he finally asked.

Madame burst out laughing, Well-Well shuddered with fright, César slowly went away, took refuge in the stable where the foal that he wanted to give to Gwen nestled its head into his hand. Gwen was awaiting him, leaning out her window; she saw Fritz arriving.

'But you said that César would be coming, that he had something to ask me. *What then?*'

The cousin was discreetly tugging his corset busk, imitating the handsome officers who would parade in front of the emperor wearing his ample Valkyrie's coat and heading for the Hofkapelle accompanied by his sister Freia from whom he had twelve sons.

'So you have come back from the Germanies, Fritz,' Gwen's father said. She was pale, her front teeth were unsightly, a pale golden curl on her shoulder, and wholly César's love; if there had only been a minute more, as Adolphe was slowly cleaning his fingernails and if he had had just as many as six fingers on each hand, like Queen Mab, César would have had enough time to arrive, but he took too long to extricate himself from the lake, his footsteps over the sand filled his shoes with water, he wouldn't have been able to enter the parlour with his drenched shoes and announce that he was going to marry Gwen, a golden curl on her shoulder, a little dark-blue silk apron around her skinny waist. And did he really want to arrive before Adolphe? And, in the past, to arrive before Eugène had proposed to that young fly-eyed girl, her white gloves full of wet sand? He could easily have shaken up his godfather and the relatives from the Franche-Comté crowding up at the gates of the ball . . . Now having taken refuge in the stable, he was looking for the image of the past in the depths of the tawny and black liquid manure. 'Where are the children? They aren't dead, one would have known so otherwise, where are the children? Ah, when that false policeman has left, we'll discuss the situation, I'm the eldest child after all.' But Mélanie's father stayed for dinner, bringing his cup to his lips while raising his little finger as he had seen his wife do. 'Well,' he said while groping for his handkerchief in the tails of his suit coat. 'Well, we'll need to think about a trousseau. And about the wedding, the guests, and all that.' 'My God,' thought the wedding guests, 'look at that pastor in his pulpit—wouldn't you say his head looks like a cat's?' Indeed, the pastor who married Mélanie had given such low bows to the rich wife of Joseph Dimanche, the owner of the manor, that he lost his head. 'My God, the pastor has lost his head,' the so-called lady of the manor thought while fanning herself. 'The reverend minister has lost his head,' repeated in turn the sanctimonious old women behind the revolving door with coloured glass panels. Since he was supposed to go back home and have tea with his wife who, standing at the parsonage window, was searching the horizon with her sea binoculars to spot the rich children with their white overshoes, he indeed had to find a head to replace the one that had rolled under the carpet-covered settee of the guardroom and that the lady of the manor had left there as a trap for Mariette, the girl from the canton of Uri, the niece of Isabelle's last suitor; he picked up this cat's head with slanting eyes and bristly eyebrows that one long saw on Élise's rubbish pile between a mopping cloth that was still in fine condition, for Élise was a spendthrift, the jam bucket that was used as a seed-bag, and those green stems which, when a child plucks one, become a trumpet but, after he discards it and an adult picks it up, holding it in his age-swollen hand, is a mere pump-kin stem. Sometimes when César is weeping over Gwen in the stable and is ready to leave for the Maison d'En Haut, if he raises his eyes one last time to the window, towards the faceted thick drinking glass and the cast-iron, snake-shaped candlestick, he happens to hear a faint sound of green trumpets in the village. The children! But he hurries over in vain. To come back to the pastor, when his flock saw him with his cat-like head, they didn't allow themselves the slightest remark, only little Paul, who was being given a bath in front of the window, pointed with his curved rosy finger at the pussy-cat going by. Was it also his fault that he had lost his mind in front of the horse merchant's rich wife?

'You will be allied with the powerful of this world,' would repeat to him back then, at charity sales, the old maid who was a graphologist and stamp-collector and awaited customers on the threshold of her fabric shop, her purpled hands enclosed in filoselle gloves. But it's Amélie. The laundress of Fraidaigue! The woman who had been rather insane! How small the world is.

'A magnificent line of good fortune, wealth, success.'

Thus, whenever a new parishioner settled in the area, followed by a wagon of furniture and a few skinny horses, 'Alfred, aren't they,' the pastor's wife would ask haltingly, 'aren't they rather poor?' At this last word, her voice would lower. She wanted her own children to play and amuse themselves in a public garden with the rich people's children who wore white overshoes on rainy days; she constantly blew her shallow little nose, which was wearing down little by little; and instead of collecting, like Zoé at the Maison d'En Haut, butterfly wings to make a coat, she would keep watch, from afar, on the English governess leading the children who were taking their most beautiful toys so that the disdainful babies in white overshoes would like them. As soon as the pastor's wife had spotted the rich children with her sea binoculars, her own little children would need to have their clothes put on, fast, fast, and leave. But, alas, all the nanny would do is go round in circles, without locating the foreign children, since she was unable to find her bearings because of her flat black eyes, deprived of that homing-pigeon eyelid that they pull down in front of the sun, their secret enemy. She would wander at random through the garden; have I already seen this piece of bread covered with dust? Once, in the past, when she got lost in the Hampton Court maze, she constantly went back and forth in front of a dusty little piece of bread fallen from the hand of a tired traveller who had been walking around for miles between the yew hedges. To no avail, she would sometimes turn to the right, sometimes to the left, a song from Purcell's Wednesday-evening Tenebrae service was playing, to no avail, behind the hedges. It was the Easter bank holiday, Jim was waiting outside, a woman's hat on his head, his fist on his hip, and it was only a half-day later that she was saved by the captain of the maze who came up on the bridge and guided her so that she could go back home on the train, its red velvet seats blackened by the smoke of the island and crammed with a thousand tennis players. At last she would find the children in white overshoes, let herself drop on a bench, and weep. Heavy horses would be galloping around the public garden. The horse dealer was standing at the tower window, a whip around his neck, feeling encumbered with his big ruddy hands used to slapping the rumps of his horses; whenever the servant women saw him striding into the hallways, they'd put their hands on their derrieres. He would observe the lands of creation from the tower— the horses gallop over it every which way, separating the water from the lands, making puddles beneath their hooves. In the spring, the piles of horse drop- pings open up and give birth to lavender-blue butter- flies. But on that day, the first of autumn, on the hillsides, the coltsfoots were lifting their thin yellow- haired heads. Mélanie was getting married. With, as the servant women were gossiping with one hand on their buttocks while whispering behind the other hand all wrinkled from doing the laundry, that boy from the south, that green carabineer who, when taking a walk, would have to limp through the horse country because of the puddles created by their fabulous hooves. 'Well, well, the neighbour is back in his tower with his spy- glass. You should have waited to get married, Mélanie, until I had finished planting the thuja hedge. Well, I told you so. And that César? Will he even come? Already down there at Fraidaigue I barely noticed him, he was always down at the shore of the lake or in the stable. All the same, it's strange.' Madame sitting like a city in the little black-and-green train, Adolphe and Eugène, all of them were waiting for César, who failed to show up, the train chugged by Gwen's house, he had preferred to walk along the beach and arrive a few hours later in the horse country rather then see her windowsill from which the pink and blue pebbles had vanished ever since the arrival of the corseted cousin. The lake was washing up on the shore humble brown-striped shells unworthy of being placed by Mélanie on the lower shelf of the pedestal table between the Saint-Gallen guipure-lace curtains; César's polished shoes brought water into the sand, reconciling contraries, where, then, were the children? Gwen noticed that the wet traces left on the windowsill by the lake pebbles were fading away for ever. 'So what about that César?' her father was asking, still hopeful. Standing at the window, they were watching César, far away, walking down the beach, his head bowed, trudging through water and sand. While Madame's city-like face, Strasbourg or Amiens on an excursion, was looming in silhouette behind the portiere. Mélanie's family were gathering to welcome them on the plat-form invaded by meadow grass that sprouted up within their properties while the horses were resting; a man armed with a hoe incessantly defended the wretched asphalted rectangle; it was autumn, at the same time as the blue and rosy lake was becoming grey and green, the meadow was yellowing and the horses were galloping over it for the last time, but when they saw that city with its snowy staircases getting down from the train, they leant their long heads on the fences, neighing with astonishment.

'Well, well. The whole family. Except for your brother César? How strange. Will that brother one speaks of while laughing uncomfortably finally come?'

'What if he claimed his share now,' Eugène had said at Fraidaigue in the next room, after the marriage proposal, thinking he was whispering.

'Shut up,' Madame had retorted sharply.

And much more loudly they had spoken about something else while Well-Well, his hands joined over his poplar walking stick, was listening to the sound, coming from who knows where, of branches rustling in the wind.

'Oh, all he loves is his stable,' Madame said later. 'When you look for him, he's always in the stable. Or with his nephews. Oh, he adores Abraham, that you have to grant him. And he lives in clover, six months here, six months there.'

César! César! When he arrives in the horse country, he seems to hear voices calling out to him. Is that still Gwen at her window, with three motionless people

131

behind her, Fritz, the father who speaks English in front of the servants—'*Let's go, oh it's like butter it's a treat*'? César! César! Children are walking below a too-new tower, blowing into their green trumpets. While Madame, sitting between Mélanie's parents, was smiling scornfully and replying nothing, like a brutish woman.

'Oh, César?' Adolphe was saying, 'He's a poor fellow. And yet when our mother was still alive—she died while we were children,' he explained to Mélanie —'César was the favourite.' Red hair tenderly pressed against that grey-feathered skirt! 'Anyway . . . ' he said in a bold, virile tone, shrugging his shoulders.

That César, Mélanie's father was wondering anxiously, what if César claimed his share in lands and houses? He was brooding over this at the church where the cat-headed pastor officiated. Sitting on the last pew, César was watching a distant thick silhouette beneath a tulle veil lit up by a ray of blue-and-red sunlight. Galloping all around the church, the last judgement could be heard approaching; the fog was already rising from the earth, the sun was yellowish-green, orangey. It was only in the lower room, during this lunch where Well-Well was cooking slowly with the others, that Mélanie noticed César shyly leaning against the wall, his red bangs drooping down over his forehead, near the upright piano surmounted with two empty vases painted with purple reeds. A human being who was five-foot-six in height, and almost as wide when his arms were stretched, and a thousand times more precious than a flow of pure gold!

They are severely interrogating him: 'So when's your wedding, César?' And the stomachs plopped down on knees are jolting like animals. The tulle-draped iron wire is trembling on Mélanie's head, she constantly seems to be apologizing because her breasts are tumultuous and her thighs streaked with blue bruises, her shadow-ringed blue eyes are filling with tears. The seamstress is munching noisily in the kitchen, her muffled voice audible from the lower room teeming with walnut trees fashioned out of arms, legs, in seats, negative images of seated human beings. Hey, César, what do you think about this new sister-in-law? Hey, César? And you, César, when's your wedding? Madame is sitting there enthroned, stone staircases rising on her head, oh, isn't some European city missing? 'When's your wedding, Monsieur César?' the cat-headed pastor innocently asks. His wife has hidden her sea binoculars in her blouse; she's sighing while looking at the window; where are those children with their white overshoes? Where are those children, where are they? Adolphe is laughing, his gold tooth can be seen, he adjusts his pince-nez: 'César . . . '

'Shut up, shut up, all of you.' César grasped one of the andirons, brandishing it at the wedding party. Mélanie's mother's purplish hand covered her open mouth, the men set down their cigars, looking annoyed, Adolphe stood up to stretch his legs, his two hands passing behind the two coattails of his coat formed a small mourning table below his back. César tossed down the andiron, which bounced like a ball, and he left the room without anyone paying attention to him, only Mélanie pulled her veil down over her face and started crying. The sky darkened for a moment, creating in the room one of those nights that last no longer than an insect's short life.

'Well, say what you wish, your brother is a strange human body.'

'He drinks,' Madame said softly. 'He lives in the stable. When you enter it after he has left for the Maison d'En Haut'—she directed an encouraging nod to Mélanie: What? What? her father was wondering—'when you go into the stable, what do you see? A glass with the dregs of some Villeneuve or Dézaley wine left in the bottom. For Monsieur insists on drinking bottled wine.'

They were all a little drunk, wisps of smoke were rising from the construction on Madame's head, the room was sinking beneath the increasing weight of the men, fortunately meals come to an end, for otherwise guests would descend all the way to the centre of the earth.

'He drinks,' Madame was simply repeating.

Then she shifted the conversation to architecture and sculpture. 'Reliefs in the round, do you see what I mean?' Her big white hands were rising and hollowing out the air.

César was walking along the limit of the high grass, the sun was sinking into the horizon, placing two forefeet on the edge of the meadow, the hind legs and tail with which the sun sweeps the sky during end-of-October evenings could already be made out. But above the lake the sun is a big gold rose. Farewell Gwen, your golden curl the angel will grasp! And your voice that I won't hear any more! Nothing will be left for me but the sky, the stable, my secret abode. César lifted his eyes, but here the firmament was a great, multistoreyed machine, the night coming on little by little, effacing everything, the cords, the vast curtains held by tiebacks as big as a country. The horses were galloping in the soft soil, their manes fraying into clouds, not so long ago the world consisted only of neighing clouds amid the silence of the universe. In front of the house, the procession of Mélanie's posses- sions was getting ready, the deaf seamstress thinking of her Gamba, of her Carlino, was sitting all the way on top, on a golden armchair. César saw from afar the big tree trunks whose tails were sweeping the road, he left without saying anything in order to arrive at Fraidaigue before Mélanie's trousseau. But what was the use of that now? The cousin in his corset was rocking back and forth on the terrace, the lake violently rolling its pebble flowers. Gwen met up with César in the village street that leads to the fishnets that raise their wall of haze between the sky and the water.

'You weren't there, César?'

'I was marrying a brother.'

With her small hand placed on a stone flowered with moss, her golden curl on her shoulder, she held on to the wall so that the slightly sloping street wouldn't sweep her down to the nets. They were harvesting. Let them harvest! The wine-grower was sticking two dahlias into this oilcloth cap. Hearing the word 'marriage', she blushed. With his hands behind his back, César was kicking hard at the wall and removing some of the moss-covered stones.

'You know, I was waiting for you the other day.'

'My brother was getting engaged.'

'But my father was also waiting for you. And you went away. Where were you going without saying anything?'

'To my brother's wedding. Far from here. He's going to take the Maison d'En Haut, where else would he be able to go?'

'But I was waiting for you.' After a few moments she added, 'So was my father.'

He slowly walked off, she remained standing near the wall, grasping it with her two arms and squeezing herself so tightly against it as to bruise herself against the stones still warm from the summer. 'Gwen! Gwen!' her languid mother was shouting, letting the lacy train of her dress drag across the gravel of the terrace. Let them call me! Let them harvest!

'At bottom,' they were all concluding, sitting in their wicker armchairs in the last October sunlight and unable to keep from smirking, 'they in fact live in a sort of château, but they're almost peasants. And now that the other brother is married, where will that César settle, may I ask?'

Just as soon they were repeating the same words all over again. And so on and so forth until evening, when the nets were drawn back up on the shore, when the houses tilted to receive the assault of the waves were getting ready for night. Spying from her window, the messenger watched a load of boxes and luggage which was going by and on which was enthroned the deaf seamstress whose vast voice resounded for miles around. The tails of the tree trunks were shaking above the road, inhabited by insects gone astray, by red black-spotted bugs scurrying aimlessly over the surface of a world rolling through space. Watching the wagons coming laboriously down the road, turning to the right, heading back up through the countryside to the Maison d'En Haut, César was thinking that he could remove a board from the bottom of the *Danaé* and that the next day Abraham and Ulysee would go fishing. A boat from Meillerie was sailing high like a cliff, one of its sails dark, the other bright white, it was a leap year, the lake was flowing through the Pont des Machines, leaving lagoons on the shore over which swans waddled every morning on their cherry-wood legs, the fishermen would bring back a Roman vase to the château, the cook would keep it for the ashes of her knives. The convoy of furniture, tree trunks, insects and the deaf seamstress was going up into the high country via the same route that César followed every autumn, turning around to say farewell to the bare earth of the vineyards swept by the wind and raised up into volutes around the vine stocks by no plough. The valet of the Maison d'En Haut was awaiting the arrival of the newlyweds and hoisted the flag of Mélanie's region—big yellow gentian leaves, a passing horse—up a pole stuck at the angle of the terrace and decorated with green and white spiral bands; the carriage was already crunching along the gravel of the avenue, the doorman and carriage driver, who liked his job because he could see from the first-floor windows beautiful young women getting dressed and the officer of the Property Register hanging his daily shirt from the window catch, was choking with laughter on his seat at the idea of escorting to his wedding night Monsieur Adolphe who was wiping his gold-framed lorgnon on the tip of his waistcoat. The incurving double roof of the Maison d'En Haut appeared between the trees, the passing horse was flapping at the top of the flagpole, its hooves were moving over the red cloth.

'So,' said Adolphe, after clearing his voice. 'So then my sister, my only sister (there were three of us, Eugène, Zoé, and me, ah, and César of course!). Er . . . In every family there is a bête noire, right?'

Do they call César that? To take that bête noire in my arms! And she placed her hand on her tumultuous breasts.

'Zoé was abandoned by a man—the villain! She loved him, as one says. She has no longer been quite the same ever since that moment. Yes, little by little she stopped leaving the property. Oh, its big, you'll see, seventy-four acres around the house, fields and meadows here and there, even a mountain in the Jura. No vineyards, but with the diseases and the bad years, I'm the best off. So Zoé has stopped leaving the property, she works a little in the garden, she's not nasty.'

It's that he had never mentioned her to either Mélanie or Well-Well. But now that they're married in due form at the Town Hall decorated with gentian leaves, where the Public Records officer looks like a passing deer . . . Outside, galloping horses could be heard, the autumn sky was coming down so low it touched them, they were carrying away a jockey of fog on their croups, the children blowing in their green trumpets were marching around the church, they hadn't yet found the right sound—similar, enemy—to overthrow it. Now that they're married, that the wagons with the trousseau are already going up the avenue, Zoé's sad story can be told, interspersed with 'Let's don't judge.' Don't judge Zoé's lover! When, thought Mélanie, one should have made mincemeat out of him, torn all the blood and sawdust out of his head. So what was the use, among the fifteen rooms of the Maison d'En Haut—it's truly a château, she wrote to her parents—of that rifle room full of fencing masks and rapiers? With her brittle bones and bluish eye whites, Zoé had been in love with several young men among the approximately eight hundred people she had met during the first thirty years of her life—cousins, peddlers, railways and postal employees, hurdy-gurdy players, gardeners, acrobats, wine-growers. Every time that a bald man or a hunchback came through the family atmosphere and suddenly gleamed brightly, 'Oh, a husband for Zoé!' the visitors from the Franche-Comté would say. Unlike Isabelle's suitors, her suitors did not leave behind alluvial deposits, African shells, theological theses or a sculpted cow from the canton of Uri. Once the boy had gone and the story was over, Zoé would hatefully reject any memory of him. Her last suitor—she was now permanently settled at the Maison d'En Haut, Madame no longer wanting her at Fraidaigue, she watched her leave with the satisfaction that Zoé would be taking care of Adolphe's housekeeping (of course, what do Fraidaigue and the lake matter to an old maid?)—was a young man who had a waxy rosy complexion, was afflicted with corns on his feet and spent six months in the area, first at a fabric shop and then in a bank. He spoke in a muffled voice that smelled of cachou while measuring out cloth and obeying the orders of two tall lethargic old ladies, one of whom, as could be seen on her hand swollen with chilblains, wore a gold ring and was married despite her rectangular face and its mass of grey hair, while the other one, although quite similar, had not been chosen, and everyone turned their eyes away from this secret pain in this over-lit shop where the husband had just had a glass roof installed and had brought a tailor's dummy back from town. The shops were clustered around a sloping square, a peasant's house still stood between two shop windows, and just across the town limits extended fields and farms, some of which could be spotted along the stream by pushing apart the branches, others were warlike, helmeted, cloaked, on hilltops. Zoé would buy cloth for her blouses that were scalloped and embroidered with raised satin stich, Béat would measure out the cloth, winding the tread around her finger, and she would think of a ring and blush. The revolutions had just begun, didn't he look like a Russian emigrant beneath his astrakhan hat, especially when he was singing with his comrades in the evening: Dong, dong, dong, the *Bells of the Don*. During these balmy autumn evenings smelling of manure, so similar to March evenings when the fragile seasons tumble over like a house of cards, he would take off his lustre oversleeves and meet Zoé on the square, when the daylight was still standing in its reddish November clothes, its immense bonnet touching the clouds. Béat would speak of his big registers, the cloth that had come from overseas, where he would surely go one day—With her? With her? Oh my God!— Zoé would talk about her life, he wouldn't listen, letting his bored gaze wander overthe hazy meadows, slightly twisting his fleshy nose, waiting for a moment to get a word in. A triangular flight of birds was passing overhead, a big golden church appeared at the bottom of the valley, the distant blue mountains slowly started moving, the Maison d'En Haut seemed painted pink. Completely dressed in black and wearing a wing collar, Béat was walking forward, suffering from his tight shoes which, later, would prevent the arrival in Italy of the boss, the pretender to the throne; they were going down to the stream over a cartage path, the wagons were resting under the shed roof, behind the staircase the old father was raising the fish he had caught in the stream; he could hardly see any more, he should have been put away in a Lysol-scented asylum around which the useless night of the blind accumulates at five o'clock, but he kept clutching the doorjambs and imploring.

'It's going to rain,' Béat said.

He suggested taking shelter beneath a tree.

'But not a walnut tree, walnut trees attract lightning. You have beautiful walnut trees at your place, Mademoiselle Zoé.'

'But it's not my place, it's my brother Adolphe's.'

'But where's your home, then?'

'Nowhere.'

With a meditative look, he vigorously kicked a potato fallen off a wagon, muttering, 'Bugger off.'

'But you nonetheless have a home of your own,' he went on with his Bern stubbornness.

'No, it's like César, my other brother, he's a guest here and there, the others live on the two properties, they're married or engaged, you understand.'

'But you nonetheless have a share,' he repeated. He was getting annoyed, his corn hurt. She explained that she owned nothing, actually getting evermore surprised at the fact as she went on, 'oh, but they give me everything I want!', adding that she had only a few pieces of furniture in a garret, not the Louis XV chest of drawers in any case, nor the Scottish scarf. ('Zoé, you're too old for the Scottish scarf, you should let Isabelle have it, I would say.')

'Really? Really?' Béat kept saying distractedly, twisting his fleshy nose.

Meanwhile, Zoé was speaking about the lake, the beach, and the château where she had been born. The château that is not even hers! That so-called, supposed château. Did one know if it even existed? At the farthest edge of the property, his arms crossed over the hedge, César was wondering 'where are the children, where are they?' while gazing at the big golden church fading into the night. As far as one could see, the earth was burdened, encumbered, with grasses, houseleeks and graminae.

'Is that your brother over there? An oddball,' Béat said severely.

As Zoé was bringing the conversation back to her parents' château, he became so bored that—raising his boater and murmuring an excuse about 'joining some friends'—he took the grassy hillside path that passes in front of the cemetery forbidden to children and dogs. Dogs were leaning against the moss-covered wall, a little slaver trickling from their panting mouths, their forelegs dangling towards the field of rest. In a voice at once soft and loud, Béat shouted 'Bugger off' once again to a Bintje potato fallen onto the path shaped by the wagon tracks, quite unhappily going back to his room where a face flannel was drying on a string hanging across the window, and never returned. 'So what about your boyfriend, Zoé?' the visitors from the Franche-Comté would caw. Henceforth, who could be a husband for Zoé? The part in her hair slowly widened, becoming visible whenever she leant her head below the lamp and tapped like a woodpecker on her darning ball. Béat was now working in a bank agency. She entered, asked to see him. But he has left, she was told. Left? On holiday? No, he's been hired on as a secretary by the pretender to the throne (who had in fact just returned from the wedding in Edom). She could tell all too well that Béat had not yet left, that he was hiding behind a widespread newspaper held in his trembling little white hands, those fish-hands of bank employees, that he was crouching fearfully behind one of the high lecterns, his pen-pusher's pen behind his ear. The other, pimple-covered, employees would snigger as they waddled over to the window to watch her arrive. 'No, he's not here,' they would cruelly report, elbowing each other. Zoé would leave, as if drunk, staggering up the path leading to the Maison d'En Haut, where she had been forced to make room for the visitors from the Franche-Comté and move up to the attic; up there, once night had come, she would go and fetch Béat, dragging him back into her room, deaf and insensitive, like a cat going to a barn and bringing back her blind, deaf newborn kitten dangling from her mouth. She wasn't able to sleep any more, in the morning the sky would be primrose-coloured, during the daytime objects would fall out of her clumsy hands. 'But you've gone crazy, Zoé! Upon my word, Zoé is crazy. Another broken cup.' One day behind the raised newspaper, behind the yellow lecterns, there was truly no one, the employees drew aside, showed the palms of their hands, pulled their pockets inside out, thumping each other when Zoé decided to leave. Was Béat going along the lake in a train carriage? On a horse? In an automobile? Or was he hidden with the pretender to the throne and the chamberlain at the back of a wagon driven by a peasant who was wearing a loose black smock embroidered at the wrist with a white-cotton skull, and who might well be the horse dealer who, from the top of his tower, was sniggering while watching Mélanie's wedding procession passing by. The pretender to the throne left the area at the first sounds of war, they headed at night by foot to the mountain where hooded mules sleeping like bees were awaiting them, they couldn't catch them though they were no farther than rifle range, they hiked along the irrigation channel for hours without meeting up with a living soul, then at dawn they came across a harvest benediction service, a priest was coming out of a chalet, his cassock covered with wisps of straw, he was chasing off his fleas at sunrise, ears of maize had been heaped into a mountain on the fragrant close-cropped grass, rosy goat kids were frisking about between bowls of cream. 'But my feet really hurt too much,' Béat was groaning, 'I have to stop, it's my corn.' Sitting on a rock, his knees spread, the flannel stretching to the breaking point on his fat thighs, the pretender to the throne handed his sombrero to the chamberlain who cut out several discs from it, pierced a hole through the centre of each and applied them to the corn. But, alas, the carabinieri had had enough time to catch up with them, the pretender to the throne raised his hands, both hate and relief could be read on his greasy face, and Béat the scapegoat spent a few years in the gaols suspended over the canals. Arriving in Venice, Madame noticed a pyramid of pallid faces behind windows meshed over with iron bars, the dawn was giving a pink tint to the prison wall. Madame sometimes stood at the edge of the sea, leaning on a cardboard boulder and shading her regal eyes with her hand, waiting. Standing behind her, Eugène would rock back and forth, intently watching the corset stays as they showed through the cloth of the dress, Torcello barely emerging from the waters, Madame getting into a launch—'Let's don't take that vaporetto everyone takes'—and sitting next to a courtesan whose long hand, lengthened by a white handkerchief, was dangling. And this is when Madame saw her embassy attaché for the first time, sitting to her left, on the lookout for seabirds. All seaways lead to Torcello, doves, peacocks and parakeets head there every morning, slowly flying back at nightfall, circling the boat oared by a distraught old Jew. The jetty of loose rocks sagged under Madame's weight, the stranger, who had debarked before she did, lent her his hand. She met up with him again in front of the postcard booth, then in front of the church sunk into the ground. But what does he want? Do I look like an easy woman? Me? Now he's coming forward as if to speak to me while Eugène is showing shells to Ulysse and Isabelle! 'Madame,' he says, 'excuse me, will you be taking the launch back to Venice?' She moved off without replying; but so often during the long winter evenings, when Eugène dropped off to sleep in his chair, how she regretted not having replied! She moved off, the lorgnon having slipped out of her trembling hands and dangling from its opulent moiré ribbon, her feet couldn't carry her any more, she needed to sit down on a warm wall. Oh, did he know whom he was dealing with? He was surely an embassy attaché, with his polished shoes, black dress vest, Legion of Honour. She was thinking about her extraordinary childhood, about logarithms, about that first dance, about that fiacre too small for her dress and about that old man who accompanied her. She had been quite wrong to accept Eugène so quickly. Yet the attaché was not in the launch going back, and she saw him only once thereafter, whirling his cane on the Piazza del Duomo where countless footsteps can be heard all night long. Would he be able to find her address? She remained standing at the door of the train carriage, her rump, pushed along by the flow of travellers, swaying for a moment then recovering its usual position. The respectful stranger failed to show up. Once they had returned home, Zoé went to spend some time at Fraidaigue, where she was greeted by a big marble washbasin and Semiramis sitting on a velvet settee. She came back from there crazy. Success for Madame at last. It must be said that it was a conversation with Eugène that gave Zoé the idea to become crazy. With his boater pushed back on his head, he was looking despondently at the diseased currant bushes.

'Say, Eugène, I'd like to leave. Far from here. You, you have the children, your household. As for myself, I'd like to leave.'

She weighed hardly anything, wasn't sinking at all into the heaped-up dirt where she was standing and where he had just earthed up the dwarf beans.

'You're crazy, Zoé,' he replied distractedly, turning towards the current bushes his big face, painted by Raphaël, which rosacea had begun to attack at the same time as it did the portrait of Aunt Jean, so terrifying with her opaque breasts beneath her black blouse. César could be heard raging against the little servant who soon surged forth from the stable, his arm raised to protect his freckled face.

'What a cross!' murmured Eugène. 'And yet living in clover. Six months here, six months there. And you too, Zoé. And you'd like to leave? With what money, may I ask?'

Then it was Amélie, the linen maid, a humble tool, who spoke:

'Have you seen how she looks at you? It makes me go crazy. And doesn't it make you crazy, too? All the more so in that I have myself already been confined.'

The tip of her tongue came out of her mouth and discreetly imitated a scissoring movement.

'Oh, and what was it like?'

'Good. They took good care of me, and everything. I forgot my sorrows, like when you have a drink. As one says. Not me of course.'

'You're crazy, Zoé,' Eugène kept repeating at noon. 'Leave. But for where? With your frail health? For you're fragile, fragile,' he repeated indulgently.

Her finger in a book, Madame broke in:

'Yes, in her case, the excitation exceeds the lesion.'

A doctor had just come to stay at Fraidaigue during the fifteen days of his military service. He would sit at their table, his pale blue shirtfront kept in place by means of golden fasteners. One spoke humbly to Madame, one asked her to pass the salt, to pour the water, she raised her walled-up-woman's big, lividly white hand to impose silence, she was hanging on the lips of the doctor, her toenails quivering in her thick boots embossed with bunions.

'How right you are, I've always been interested in medicine, I . . . '

That is, in order to forgive them, you have to imagine Madame's parents, if she actually had a childhood —it's not proven that she did—before the evening of the ball when a father was walking on the pavement while holding the glove full of wet sand that the fiacre held out to him. Worn out by the work bench, the hard winters, how would they have found the energy to explain to the gigantic young woman that one needs to show consideration for ordinary creatures, to pass them the bread, the salt, and not run them through with a regal stare. She was raising her hand to impose silence, remarking coquettishly, 'I think I would have made a very good doctor.' The doctor bowed, thought the tarragon-flavoured chicken was quite tasty, he who had had such a difficult childhood, his socks falling down over his shoes and the white-cotton ribbons hanging down from his pants in a way that betrays a boy without a mother. As soon as he had left, Madame said about Zoé, 'In her, the excitation exceeds the lesion.'

'You're fragile, Zoé,' added Eugène.

'But I could nonetheless do something.'

'But what? You're crazy, Zoé.'

Towards evening, Madame, who was hastily cleaning her fingernails, finished what Béat, Eugène and Amélie the laundress had started. She was staring at the dirty camisole that was hanging past Zoé's blouse. Eugène slipped onto the wooden balcony and, after falling asleep, awoke with a big red stain on his cheek, a spider had dashed up from the violet-strewn lake and crossed his face while he was sleeping. Sometimes the water that strikes the walls of Fraidaigue imperceptibly withdraws while the moon remains suspended like an enormous yellow globe at the horizon.

'But stay here, Zoé, where are you going?'

Zoé sat down on the green rep chair crossed with a mustard-yellow lace insert that she had embroidered in the past, before the arrival of Semiramis.

'I'm looking at you,' Semiramis was thinking aloud, 'as the stars must look at the earth. I think of so many things—literature, architecture, hygiene. But I don't want to say anything, I'll die without having said anything at all . . . So, Zoé, your lover?'

Gazing at her knitting, she was almost smiling. Ah, if she could only keep her eyes lowered she would be like the others, a face topped off with a snowy construction, but, after all, it was merely a chignon. Zoé almost reached out to touch it.

'So, Zoé, your lover? My little finger told me.'

She looked obligingly at her fat white thumb. Zoé shook her head, holding back her tears.

'You mean you don't have any news?'

But of course she did. Oh, he would write to her, begging her to leave with him. 'But me, leave the Maison d'En Haut, Adolphe who needs me so much?' She placed a hand on her skinny bosom. 'He's leaving for America.'

He was indeed packing, his pen behind his ear, but in order to leave with the future king.

'Oh, he writes me such beautiful letters!'

She had also written to him once, the most beautiful love letter in the world, and then tossed it into the sewer below the Maison d'En Haut.

'Ah, Zoé, really?' Madame said calmly, her eyes still gazing at her knitting, 'he loves you that much? You're quite lucky, Zoé!'

And after a moment of silence, as if the idea had just come to her, 'But then why doesn't he marry you? What's preventing him from doing so? I don't think he's a minor. And you, Zoé, it seems to me that you haven't been underage for a long time.'

She was smiling. She put her knitting on her mighty knees and looked at Zoé.

Zoé . . . No, he didn't write to her and never would. He was going away, but to Spain, had asked nothing of her, didn't love her, not at all. The heavy look was weighing ever-more heavily, it could have been evaluated in milligrams, in centigrams, it was the heaviest thing in the world. Zoé burst into tears.

'Ah, ah,' said Madame with satisfaction, 'it's not so brilliant then?'

Zoé fell from the tightrope with her poor brittle bones, her bluish eye whites, her dull thinned-out hair that no longer enveloped her in a cloak as it once had. She fell, as did Benjamin who had rubbed his little feet in the chalk before he also stepped out on the tightrope, ending up in the virgin forest, his wife, at the door of their hut, futilely waving the purple scarf that concealed her goitre. Zoé started ripping up her hand-kerchief. 'But you're going crazy, Zoé!'

'No, I'm not crazy, only in despair, but, after all, why shouldn't I go crazy? I'd escape all their dirty pity.' And she tore out handfuls of the fringe around the tiger rug that had been brought back by Benjamin to spread beneath Isabelle's feet and that Madame placed under the piano stool that tilted to the side and cracked like a ship.

'Your sister Zoé has become crazy,' Madame wrote to Adolphe, struggling to hold the penholder in strong white hands that could still grasp big objects, plates, a stick, but no longer thin needles, no longer moths. 'But she's mildly insane, it's not dangerous, you'll be able to busy her with small tasks. She's been de-stringing beans here, it's the preserves season.'

The ransom was thus chores, de-stringing beans, stoning plums for jam, but she could always abandon such work, go over and sit down in a flowerbed. Through the grimy windowpane of the stable, César would watch his little sister plunging her hands into

155

the earth, a strange form of relief for a tormented soul. Earth! Earth! César was leaning his forehead against the horse which suddenly moved off to roll over in an area where there was room. Zoé left on foot for the Maison d'En Haut, without luggage, her hair all ruffled up; she walked past the corner from which the lake disappears, at which César would stop every autumn and call out 'Gwen! Gwen!' in vain with his migrating bird's voice. Rather annoyed, Madame was knitting on the velvet settee; reducing Zoé, with her brittle bones, to powder had been too easy when one thinks of Eugène who remained sound of mind, although he had taken up the habit of sleeping in that little room behind the kitchen—'it'll be more peaceful for you that way, darling'—and often taking refuge on the wooden balcony to sleep in the sunlight. Who knows whether he hadn't in fact beckoned to that spider with his rheumatism-crippled finger, for it had dashed over those violet-strewn waters that lap against the beach and leave the centre of the lake pure and vast. The peddlers leaning against the door and holding the basket of Sunday rolls on their stomachs would flee once they had been run through by Madame's stare, and they could then be seen running down the beach, meeting up with the messenger bringing back the gold-headed needles in her wicker cart. As for Adolphe, he escaped as soon as he could, married Mélanie with her tumultuous breasts and rarely took the road heading back down to Fraidaigue. Now that the two Rims had been annihilated by their ruin and the loss of their beautiful gold-and-ivory-inlayed secretary desk, that Benjamin-Dogodala had vanished in the virgin forest, and that Eugène had taken refuge on the wooden balcony, 'If you wish to come out on it as well, darling, but I think it would be prudent to have it reinforced, two people, you understand . . . ,' the only one left was César. 'What can he be made of that resists me so? Wood? Leather? Tinder fungus?' Madame could look him up and down all she wished, he would simply sit down near the fireplace, leave, come back inside, go off to the stable. But it's said that by the time Madame is dead—if she ever dies, if César kills her with a pitchfork in the stable or invites her to go fishing after removing a board from the bottom of the *Danaé*—all the villagers will have taken up the habit of staring at one another; that the weaklings will writhe in despair and end up vanishing; that the astonished circus people, their cold-reddened legs sticking down from their sequined costumes, standing for the parade and facing the gathered villagers who are staring at their necks, at their stomachs, will slowly retreat into their canvas abodes and nail back onto the bottom of their boxes the bride who lets her sewn hands dangle, the notary, the woodcutter and Death. But for the time being, Madame was alive and flourishing, while Mélanie and Adolphe, duly married, were heading at their horse's pace up the avenue between the sycamores.

'So, Zoé . . . ', he was saying, shrugging his shoulders, 'keeps searching for new names for herself, Diaphane, for example. She writes them on walls, wrapping paper, tablecloths, the snow, but besides that? . . . Here's Zoé.'

Gazing at her brother was that wrinkled forehead, those additional eyes at the end of a gold chain. Ah, she really was crazy because it was that which had replaced one of the lake children! She moved off without greeting Mélanie, a rough blue cotton apron around her waist, and began walking along the wall of peach trees.

'She doesn't like these surroundings, it's agoraphobia.'

'When César comes,' he continued, 'she seems happier.'

'Your brother César, you mean he comes?'

'Every six months, as soon as it's autumn. Oh, he won't bother you, we hardly see him. He's an oddball,' he added severely.

They were entering the big wood-panelled room at the back of which was an emerald-green stove and, on the ceiling—in case of freezing temperatures—a tap for emptying out the newly installed bathtub upstairs. A thread from a spiderweb was grazing Adolphe's already bald skull, he shooed it off. And now a fly? He shooed it off, it came back stubbornly; he sat down in front of the fire.

César thus spent six months of the year at Fraidaigue, six months at the Maison d'En Haut. One needed to support his personality. 'First of all, because he's our brother ... Let's not judge. Then because if he asks for his share—fortunately, he doesn't even think about it, I assure you, at Fraidaigue he spends hours lying on his back, in the grass, on the beach or on the vineyard dirt, gazing at the sky, or else he goes to the very back of the stable and beats the little manservant.' He was a *minus habens*, a wretched human being.

He laughed very softly while wiping his lorgnon on the tip of his waistcoat.

'All the same, if he got the fancy of getting married ... '

'Oh, does he have plans?'

'Plans? But my dear Mélanie! Who would want that *minus habens*? Nonetheless, that's the sword of Damocles hanging over our heads, as my sister-in-law says, our sister-in-law, my dear. Let's not judge.'

But when would César be coming?

He neglected to answer that question, she was blushing, raising her hand to her tumultuous breasts, he was showing her around the house, 'your house, my dear', with sudden courtesy. If only he wouldn't constantly take off his lorgnon! Mélanie kept turning away from his eyes crumpled like those of newborn babies.

'Here's his room. He comes here as soon as the grapes are harvested. Put your mind at ease, you still have a long month before his arrival. Here, from November to March, there is wood to cut, tools to repair. It's not in fact very fair that he always spends the winter here and the summer at Fraidaigue, now that workers cost so much to hire and can rarely be found. But what else would you expect? He loves the vineyard so. We are very keen about his happiness, he's our brother, the eldest child. When our mother was living—she died a long time ago, have I already told you?—he was definitely her favourite child. We don't know why he likes staying at the farm so much, we hear him shouting at the little manservant, don't you bother with all this, my dear, it's our cross. And yet he's lucky! Anyway, let's not judge.'

The trousseau procession was moving laboriously up the avenue, the deaf seamstress walked over to Mélanie, heehawing and moving her head up and down like a horse. 'I will never see those horses again!'

Only one will trot from the stable to the fountain. Perched on its back, Émile, the ward of the commune, bearing scars from César's blows, is laughing, his white teeth showing in his filthy little face. Too big for the boxwood flowerbeds and the oval fountains, the tree trunks had to be relegated to the stream bank and the larvae and red bugs rehoused on the terrace wall where they thereafter lived among the leaves of the maidenhair ferns. Even here, at the Maison d'En Haut, the little ogre's old house whose lunar side was becoming visible, even here, there was maidenhair fern! As there was on the ruined tower that Armand finished demolishing during that famous haze-enveloped night when the crashing of the stones mixed with that of the waves.

'But isn't it still the harvest season?' Mélanie was asking. 'It seems so cold.'

It was snowing on the unfortunate harvested grapes; the carriage entrance was closed after the wine had been brought in.

'So, César,' Madame said kindly while unwinding a needle from her chignon, 'they must be waiting for you up there. How well you will be taken care of by that nice new sister-in-law. No, no, César, don't protest. New is always better.'

Bent over her knitting, she chuckled softly for she had just received from Adolphe a letter that she was hiding in her embroidery basket. 'Dear sister,' he said, 'since Mélanie has just arrived at the Maison d'En Haut, don't you think that we could stay alone this winter and that César remain at Fraidaigue? Of course, it's however you wish, naturally, but we already have Zoé, she doesn't want to trim her fingernails any more. What a model for the parish!' She couldn't bear the number 2, nor the word *if*.

'. . . But,' Mélanie was asking, 'isn't César . . . your brother . . . going to be arriving soon?'

'In fact, darling, I have a surprise for you. Since it's our first winter together, he'll remain at Fraidaigue. Our sister-in-law kept insisting on that, and I thought it would make you happy. Moreover, they have some casks that need fixing and the winepress to clean up. I thought that you'd prefer staying alone with me. His shouting in the stable, if you only knew! He's our cross.'

For the last time, César was standing on the beach near the *Danaé* which was bobbing in the water; the lake was rising, the sky descending nearly all the way to it, the living world was gripped between the jaws of a pair of pliers, a great triangular bird formation was gliding across that hardened sky without cutting into it.

'The moment has come, he's going to leave,' remarked Eugène, who was making draught excluders for the windows, 'we'll have our peace and quiet, won't we, darling?'

Madame looked at him. 'Have you already forgotten?' She was speaking in a soft, affectionate, slightly worried voice. 'That letter from Adolphe . . . César is spending the winter here.'

Eugène blushed. 'No one ever says anything to me,' he muttered.

César left, gripping his small wicker suitcase full of his fustian jackets and, on top of them, the shaving mirror that he hangs up in the stable. Crackling like a military corset, the suitcase reminded him of Fritz. 'Gwen!' he shouted in a voice similar to the squealing of migrating birds.

'A better room for that *minus habens*? You don't find his room good enough for him? What? A room looking out to the south? For another year, you say? But you don't really mean that, my dear.'

Irritated and standing on the threshold of the Maison d'En Haut, Adolphe was rocking back and forth on his rubbery feet.

'Look, your César's arriving! We're going to tell him that he can just turn around and go back.'

César emerged onto the avenue where the children, in the past, armed with their bird calls and decoys, would try to capture a bird and take it back to the little ogre, surrounded by the visitors from the Franche-Comté and fattening up on the terrace. They would equip themselves with their green trumpets, march in a big circle around the Maison d'En Haut, searching for that similar, enemy, sound that would make it collapse.

'But darling,' Eugène was saying, 'shouldn't he have been told, so that he wouldn't go up there for nothing? . . . No, no, excuse me, you're always right. Yes, yes, darling . . . And yet . . .' he was whispering, like Galileo, once the door had closed on her majestic rump.

'And so, César'—Adolphe was barring the entrance to the house—'didn't my letter arrive at Fraidaigue? And yet I sent it the day before yesterday. I wrote that Mélanie and I would prefer staying alone this winter. After all, it's our honeymoon.'

He chuckled while wiping off his lorgnon on the tip of his waistcoat.

'There are apparently some casks that need fixing down there. They were laying claims on you and I gave in. But wait, César, don't go off like that. César!'

The nomad, the D.P., made an about-face, headed down the avenue without looking back.

'The least I should have done is offer him something to drink,' he muttered irritatingly. 'And you, my dear, where were you? What's done is done, he's going away. I regret not having offered him a glass of plum brandy.'

While César was walking down to Fraidaigue, the iron sky softened, a gleam gave a tawny tint to the clouds. 'And so, César, you're already back?' shouted Madame, who was looking out for him at her window. He pushed his hat back on his head and, without answering, took a shot at the woodpile. She began guffawing with her equinox laugh, the messenger shuddered, a few poor windowpanes fell out, the glazier hastily left his workshop in the neighbouring town. So César would stay at Fraidaigue that winter, watch the lake turning grey, the iron rising to the surface, gone the light pebbles that he would place on Gwen's windowsill at dawn. She had just got married, was leaving with Fritz who had really donned his corset this time, comrades were holding their swords crossed above their heads, her blond curl was flowering on her shoulder, where was César? Lying on the beach, like that day when Well-Well was coming down from the train station, he was gazing at the sky slowly coming closer to the earth. On its immense back, the lake was carrying a boat from Meillerie on which a fisherman wearing a blue vest was coming out of his cabin and stretching in the hazy, biting, November air. César was still chewing over the affront that he had just endured, his departure from Fraidaigue now that the harvesting was finished, while Madame—who had truly seemed to be watching him leave, to be laughing, he had glimpsed those deep-sea-diver teeth—was hiding Adolphe's letter in her embroidery basket under an old letter from her own father and a gnawed-off pencil.

'Here's what Adolphe was writing to me, César,' she said the first evening. 'Do you want to read it, César? Whatever you wish . . . ' while he was sitting in front of the fireplace and listening, without turning his head, to the noise of gurgling water audible through the crackling of the fire. After all, if he got married? He had the right to do so, he was the eldest child. The engineer's daughter in her houseboat? The Seventh-Day Adventist's daughter? Thomas' niece who tidied up her uncle's garden every day? The next day, on the beach, he distractedly kept picking up lake pebbles. 'This is what all the rocks of the world will end up becoming, isn't it?' the children would think, their hands full of light pebbles that could make twenty ricochets across the water. Their little faces were becoming more distinctly visible. César took a grey pebble, then a pink one, then a blue one, and arranged them into a circle.

A green mouse
Scurrying through the little grass

I pick him up by the tail
Show it to these gentlemen
Ap pi apple of gold
The prettiest one will have to go out

The engineer's daughter! What a pity. She was tall, shapely, solemn.

Pim pi pom d'or.

Thomas' niece, who would tidy up her uncle's garden, now she's out. She'd have liked to have him, as Isabelle would later say. Poor Isabelle! Where would she go, and Ulysse, and Abraham, Madame leading the procession, Eugène bringing up the rear and timidly carrying the pelargonium? Too bad for them. That false start—how they must have laughed among themselves!—was the last drop, the one making the cup brim over, the water flowing down in torrents into the basin placed underneath, the sky lowered even further towards the earth and the waves. Fate fell upon the Adventist's daughter. César didn't even know her first name as he watched her strolling with her parents on Saturdays, which was Sunday for those parishioners. Alas, she would then be thinking, if only I were somewhere else, if at this very moment I were entering a train carriage, if were walking along a hawthorn-lined path, I would perhaps meet the young man who would ask for my hand. Suitors withdrew like will-o'-the-wisps while she was walking down the road between her parents. César gave another chance to Madame and to the after-effects of her stroke, he kept himself from heading to the Adventist clinic. If from now to April I haven't met her . . . One day he cheated after spotting her from afar and slipping into the lane, it was one of those February days, harbingers of spring, that gallop along with their pointed bonnet, holding a long lance with a gold pommel that contains their message: five more weeks and it would be the First of April, April Fool's Day; and no more Adventist's daughter in sight than on my empty hand! César began playing with fire, prowling around the glassworks on the way leading to the clinic. He would leave dressed in fine black clothes, a bowler on his thick red hair, 'Where's he going? Does he go out with women?' the pale-faced servants would wonder, standing superimposed behind the barred-over window struck by only a few flakes of foam during big storms. He would avoid the ground where the tower formerly rose, ground across which Well-Well trod fearlessly and on which he would be killed beneath horses' hooves some three years later, and across which Madame herself walked on her big feet bunion-bumpy feet, an act that could indeed cause her atrocious death in a rowboat. César was taking the same way to the station that Well-Well had come down in order to agree to Adolphe's marriage proposal. Ah, if only he had hurried a little more that day! If only he had torn off more quickly that striped snail hanging from his red bangs! Let's don't think about that any more. Does one marry for love?, the old uncle widower would snigger while trying to fry some eggs on a still hot overturned flatiron. Here's the Adventist's daughter! My God, here she is! This time it's impossible to avoid her, the die is cast, idiot, why did I come this way? The whole world extends the other way. There's only one thing left to do, to be careful not to ask her hand in marriage. She was coming back from town, going to take the avenue leading to their clinic, but her garter came unstitched, forcing her to hide for a few minutes behind the hedge to pin it back up, and that's how she ran into Monsieur César! She was carrying a big package, they were too poor to pay the messenger and they were right in doing so, since no one ever knew exactly what role she played for the inhabitants of Fraidaigue, it was as if she prowled at night along the cornice, otherwise how would she have seen that poor wretch Eugène, according to what she told her dear friend Ol' Miss Gibaude, hanging by his belt from a hook on the evening of César's wedding night and Madame smiling, with one foot forward, her hands behind her back? This is apparently what she saw in their bedroom.

'What are you doing here?' César asked stupidly.

'I'm taking a stroll,' she said, concealing her package.

'You're lucky.'

'Oh, it's my father who baptizes in the lake on Saturday mornings and my mother who takes care of the housekeeping.'

'And your pretty sister? . . . You're the eldest girl, aren't you? Wouldn't you like to set up a house with someone soon?' he continued distractedly while tracing eights with his shoe.

The girl let her package drop, clasped her hands, said, 'Oh, Monsieur César!', came closer and put her head on his shoulder. 'It was so long ago . . . But you were paying no attention to me . . . ' Because she wept easily, her eyes were green and red, but her complexion, seen from up close, was velvety.

'Monsieur César, how secretive you are!' said her mother a few moments later while shaking her finger at him in a grumbling, jesting manner; she thought she was made for getting along with young people and would pleasantly threaten them with her index finger. They'd send this threatening finger back into their dreams and awake in a sweat, just in time to hear the messenger pushing her creaking cart along the lake.

'Monsieur César, how secretive you are! But it's that you weren't paying any attention whatsoever to Blanche!'

Blanche! César shuddered. Any kind of name, Nicole or Marguerite, but not that foamy name. It was too late to pull out of it, her father was coming in, Blanche threw herself into his arms while screaming, 'I'm engaged!'

'With Monsieur César, of Fraidaigue,' her mother said triumphantly. 'Papa, pour us a little non-alcoholic wine.'

'Monsieur César,' the evangelist asked after a few moments, 'do you intend, like your brothers, to take on a property?'

'Couldn't I find a job at the glass factory? Oh, not as an employee, naturally, but as a guide taking visitors around, explaining everything?' Lady S. . . . impassive, her shopping bag full of Oberland chalets. Blanche had a pitiful expression on her face: So no château? If it's for marrying a cicerone, then I might as well not marry. But to get married . . . When one has constantly tearful green eyes, a nose that turns red, a desire to weep during the bi-millenary procession, lakeshore Celtic ancestors on the mind, and the girls scream, 'Big Blanche has tears in her eyes!'

'Be a cicerone? But why, since you have two properties?'

'But my two brothers are living in them. Yet I'll manage. If you don't mind'—he raised his hand to his head—'we can speak about this later.'

The evangelist became silent—would it be such an advantageous marriage after all?—peered above all the heads at the Henry II sideboard, his lips formed a faint smile, he turned almost transparent. This was also how, in the middle of a sermon on the lawn, he would stop, raise his hand, half-open his mouth, stare at a point on the horizon, seeming to become disembodied, everyone turning around furtively, but no, nothing, still nothing, not the slightest last judgement, no black horse on the waves, then his hand would fall back down and he would take up his sermon again.

'Blanche is engaged to Monsieur César, of Fraidaigue,' he announced casually the next morning to the little coadjutor who was doing the bookkeeping, gazing fondly at the evangelist and keeping two curled fingers hanging from his mouth which was nested at the back of a bushy beard. The squad of sick people were walking barefoot across the lawn, led by the fat baroness.

'Ah, Monsieur Alfred,' said the coadjutor, 'I'm very very happy. It's revenge.'

Revenge for what? What does he mean? That stupid little fellow? But haven't I been successful? Revenge for what? Look at these beautiful buildings, these lawns, these distinguished sick people. Would anyone else dare think that he hadn't been successful? In the evening, in their bedroom, they congratulated each other: 'To say that they could have remained in that faraway paradise, fighting against the absinthe that they're harvesting, pressing and distilling secretly, and whenever the pastor leaves a house, laughter can immediately be heard, and Joseph Dimanche with his big whip around his neck . . . ' Why has that fellow just spoken about revenge?

'Where will they live?' that idiotic coadjutor asked again.

When César returned to Fraidaigue, 'But where's he coming from? Does he go out with women?' wondered the servants behind the barred-over windows.

'I have an inkling,' Madame was saying, sitting on the velvet settee, 'that he's no longer thinking about getting married. He has understood. Oh, thanks to me! He has behaved himself all this winter that he has been spending here. He could have held a grudge against us, after all, for having to come back down from the Maison d'En Haut . . . Stop rocking back and forth! And to say that all my life long you've let me torment myself about that marriage! I myself knew that he adored his nephews, but I didn't want to say anything. Shut up, he's here.'

'Here I am,' he said, standing on the threshold. 'I've just become engaged to the Adventist's daughter, the eldest daughter.'

Madame dropped her knitting needle, bent down. She was all red when she straightened back up, the heavy staircases of hair tilting towards the left.

'Ah!' she finally uttered with a hoarse breathy voice—a small stroke?—'With the eldest daughter? The one who has red eyes? César! You're getting married?'

'But I have the right to do so, I'm the eldest child.'

'Of course you do. Where will you live?'

'Oh, we'll see about that later. Let's not decide anything ahead of time.'

Eugène was rocking back and forth on his heels and tiptoes. She motioned to him to stop, slowly folded her knitting, forgot a needle in her hair, stood up. At the door: 'You can naturally do whatever you wish, César. It's not I who . . . But your mother . . . '

A sob kept her from continuing. The next morning, the breakfast tablecloth was folded over César's and Eugène's plates. Madame, who had got up at dawn, was sweeping the dining room, the broom sometimes slipping out of her big hands. 'I'll have to get used to it,' she was muttering. When she had swept up around their feet, she left the room, went up to the garret and, all morning long, she could be heard shoving trunks and suitcases around. At noon she appeared dressed in some old travelling clothes, a chequered carrick cape which, back then, her poor dead-tired mother had left in her dowry basket which was as big as a laundry hamper. While having a cup of coffee, Eugène offered wavers from a tin box 'to celebrate th's . . . th's . . . this affair . . . ' Madame pointed to the furniture with her strong white hand.

'César,' she was murmuring, 'I'm entrusting you with my parlour furniture. It needs to be brushed very softly, along the fibre of the velvet. And brushed every day. Velvet collects so much dust! Oh, how awful life is!' she suddenly shouted, 'Parlour furniture that needs dusting every day! As for the piano,' she added more calmly, 'don't forget to cover the keyboard with the white sheet that I embroidered. Back then.'

When it depended only on her to marry the doctor. The doctor? You're joking. The mayor, the general! César took refuge in the stable, a cheerful ray of sunlight coming through the open door and giving a tawny tint to the black liquid manure; he bent over it but couldn't see the past any more, the demolished tower, the stones thrown by their father on the white roses fallen off the young coffin the evening before—nor the future, the horses trampling Well-Well, Madame's horrible death in a sinking rowboat, an ageing Isabelle from whom the Scottish scarf was taken back, as it had been from Zoé. That evening he went off along the beach, dressed in fine black clothes, a drop of eau de Cologne on his handkerchief. The beings of the third day were swinging on the little waves licking the sand, he crushed the striped snail that he had torn off his hair, too late, the day that Well-Well . . . Standing at the parlour window, Madame was watching him walk away, Eugène shyly raising himself up to see a bit of the lake. She was keeping an impenetrable silence, not blaming anything on anyone. The weather was sappy and overcast, as in April, dark forest-like clouds pushed along by a few empty gusts of wind were slowly gliding by against the grey backdrop of the sky. Blanche was sweating, they were strolling side by side in the garden where the barefoot baroness was leading her cohort of sick people around one last time before nightfall.

'Do you also follow that treatment?'

'Oh, in the morning I walk barefoot through the dew to stimulate the circulation of the blood.'

Her legs were purplish. A finger pressing on them—not César's of course, not yet—left a mark.

'My father would like me to wear only belted tunics, like the others; the ones the baroness wears are made of Chinese silk. That's what my father would like. Not you?'

'No, no,' César said distractedly.

The next day, she went to the tailoress. When's the wedding? Oh my God, she had no idea. He wasn't in a hurry, or so it seemed. No, it wasn't that, but there were some problems to solve with his brothers; he was nice, so nice, he came every evening after he had taken a tour with his boat; he liked the lake so much. In any case, she'd need a dress for travelling; in a shade of grey?

'Oh, M'zelle Blanche, I don't recommend grey. You need a shade of lily and rose. No, I don't see you in grey—blondes paint themselves up with that colour.'

Blanche was placing her finger on a model, raising her eyebrows inquiringly, the tailoress shook her head no and quickly licked her index finger to turn the page. A white cashmere wedding gown would also be needed, and yet, Blanche sometimes wondered, her green-and-red eyes filling with tears, would she really get married one day? Meanwhile, César invited her to Fraidaigue.

'How's that?' he said, 'you've never been to the château?'

'I think I've never even gone near it. You see, we live on the other side of the train tracks and all the shops are around the glass factory.'

That false leaf-covered church was lit up every night, the young men, wearing a blue band on their forehead like acrobats, would grasp the burning molten glass in big pliers, the surrounding vineyards catching fire one after the other.

'This is my fiancée,' César dared to announce when leading her towards Madame, enthroned on her velvet settee. Droplets of cold sweat were dangling from the ends of Blanche's extended hands. Madame was embroidering a big curtain, her thick eyelids obstinately lowered. She didn't utter a syllable; after a few moments of silence, they noticed Eugène sitting on a little chair, he went to fetch the wine, offered wafers from a tin box. The messenger, who had caught a cold, stayed in bed that night, so no one knew what later happened in the bedroom where they slept. Meanwhile, Blanche, politely turning towards the town statue—birds leave droppings on its shoulder, the man with the Chinese hat plays music at its feet—making the settee sag under her weight, asked what she was embroidering. With her big white hands.

'A curtain,' she finally replied in a hoarse breathy voice. 'A curtain for one of the parlour windows. Four will be needed.'

'A beautiful project.'

'An immense project. It will take months, years. I want to transform the whole château. I have all sorts of plans. In my head.'

She pointed to her globe-sized head; her eyes remained lowered. César suddenly felt pity for her; the poor woman, she's failed and she feels it; the staring trick is over. It even seemed that she might smile, that one or two of her deep-sea-diver teeth could already be glimpsed.

'I'm going to create a bathroom and eliminate that big earthenware stove. Central heating. In these six-foot-thick walls!'

She chuckled softly. So was it a fact, a disappointed Blanche was thinking, that they would not have Fraidaigue? What a pity! That tower, those deep embrasures, that view of the lake . . . So it would be the Maison d'En Haut? Otherwise, she couldn't really see . . . She was chewing like a rabbit on a waver; her red-and-green eyes looked over the furniture. She looks them over, lies in wait, oh!, she won't have them, better to set this place on fire. And Madame spoke of Blanche's young sister. 'Now *she's* a beautiful girl—and so young! And she's really charming. How is it that she's not married yet? She surely has no lack of good matches.' Then she grew silent, sadly lowering her eyes on her embroidering and replying not a single additional word to Blanche's questions. After accompanying her to the threshold of the madhouse, César departed in the *Danaé*. He jumped into it after pushing it off, its bottom scraping the sand, and then the *Danaé* was drifting towards the middle of the lake. A dark-blue river cut through the middle of the lake, fish and blue algae, Savoyards with their sky-blue faces were floating on the calm waters. And what if he met up with the children standing in their little fishing rowboat! Yet he felt that his quest was over. 'If only,' he exclaimed aloud, 'it were Gwen I was marrying! But Blanche! And I don't even know how this happened. Should I have proposed to half-deaf Laura? No, I know, to no one at all because of my brothers, isn't that it?' Nothing but the noise of the oars was responding, he rowed back to the shore, opened the tower door. Madame was still enthroned on the settee, the curtain fallen to her feet had folds and stone-like cracks. She was hastily cleaning her fingernails, Ulysse was hanging about on his crutches, Abraham's flute could be heard, Isabelle was building a room with cardboard and bobbins.

'Poor little Isabelle,' she said in a low and distinct voice, once César had entered the room. 'Poor, poor innocent children!'

Isabelle raised her head.

'You'll be able to take your doll, but not your doll-house, I think.'

'Take where, Mum?' asked Isabelle anxiously.

'Your uncle César is throwing us out, my child.'

That evening she murmured to herself, 'I think I'll take my bedroom.' She was pointing at the roller beds with her strong white hand.

'But, darling, we haven't reached that point.'

'And what point have we reached?'

'I don't know . . . So much can happen.'

The next day she saw César shuddering at Blanche's name, and she thereafter broke her silence and kept repeating 'Blanche! Blanche!' for the slightest reason. She would shout out the name in the evening, the foam would respond, César would put his hands over his ears behind his green half-curtain. (The other half had been stolen by the messenger during that fatal night when the turtledove died.) But this wedding wouldn't take place, it'd be broken off one of these days, as had been his liaison with Elsy or with the shooting-gallery woman, his love for Gwen, the threat every leap year of the engineer's daughter, Thomas' niece or of the bustling Savoyard women when the lake thaws.

'Eugène,' she resolutely began the next morning, 'shouldn't the gazebo be demolished? It might as well collapse.'

She had exchanged her chequered travelling clothes for her old green dress embroidered in matching tones.

'But darling . . . '

'We'll make a modern concrete gazebo, I've already informed the architect.'

She started building. Oh! She had herself apparently mixed the concrete, spoiling the mortar. She was also planting, grabbing the shovel from the gardener who was standing there pensively, placing her big bunion-embossed foot on the spade. In her haste and anger, she had mixed up some seed, what needed to be done, good God, was sow, plant, build. Annoyed, Eugène, standing behind her, was holding flowers in a moist newspaper torn apart in places. When that Caroline Testu rose would bloom, he mused, César would be married. 'Married! We'll see!' shouted Madame. Blanche could catch scarlet fever or typhus, or fall into the lake whose waves broke against their madhouse; the garden extended like an angle into the waves, and the rich merchant would eat his meals on the nearby terrace, voices would shout 'Jedermann', the trees hatched their plots that were thwarted each time in November. Blanche could be their victim, or be run over by a train when she went to see the tailoress. 'Why don't you select grey, M'zelle Blanche. Grey is your colour.' 'There,' Madame was saying, 'I will build a rock garden with flowers sent to me from my native Jura. Ah, my father had told me so . . . ' Eugène was following her, his arms full of onions, he had lots of hobbies, his great-grandfather was the last man to climb to the vineyard with a vineyard plough on his shoulder, his grandfather was already reading Pope and Tennyson, he would envelop himself in a dressing gown in front of vine stocks burning in the fireplace, his wife would embroider the parlour armchairs in petit point.

'I think this château that has only one tower left,' Madame was saying in the evening while spraying them with saliva, 'is grotesque. I'm going to rebuild the missing tower, according to the plan, you know, of Mélanie's neighbour over in that faraway paradise. Because the fishermen still bring us lake vases, but for how much longer? This château with only one tower is grotesque.'

However, one heard the missing tower quaking when the southeast wind was blowing, as it indeed was blowing that year in July, and the fishermen suffered considerable losses. Meanwhile, Blanche was weeping, César setting up no date, the Adventist father, walking with long heron-like strides, his frightened eyes behind his glasses—Revenge for what? What did that idiotic little coadjutor mean? Hadn't he been successful? The clinic, those baronesses? Did other people perhaps think he had not been successful?—tremblingly intimated to César that Blanche wouldn't wait any longer.

'That is . . . not much longer . . . ' And he hurried off. Where would they live? The younger brother had the Maison d'En Haut, the youngest one the château. Yet perhaps they had money and could give him his share? Oh, that would be too beautiful! 'Be careful.' He sniffed with annoyance the odour of sulphur, wine and smoke floating up from those infernal regions where the children of the commune were rolling the casks sideways. Through the cellar windows came yellowish fumes that shook the houses threateningly crowded along the village streets. That evening, César rowed out towards the desperate red glimmer appearing in the east. 'Mother! Mother! If it were Gwen, I'd understand, but Blanche!' he shouted, shivering. And had he really proposed to her? The result would be the same, one of the two brothers would go off down the road; the ruthless children left their unfinished lands, walked over the waters, slowly sinking into the abyss, their hands raised. Zoé with her brittle bones and enveloped in her cloak of hair, Eugène with his big pale head, Adolphe with his already blinking eyes. They were sinking straight down, no more than their little hands could be seen, then their hands also vanished. Over the waves arose one of those strong voices that can be heard at night, it said something, then grew silent. The die were cast, Blanche was trying on dresses, the tailoress on her knees, needles in her mouth, remaining sceptical about the result. 'Oh, why did you select grey, M'zelle Blanche? You need a shade of lily and rose—blondes paint themselves up with grey.'

On Friday, Madame hired on some women and ordered them to begin the big cleaning that she, overly busy with planting and constructing, had not yet undertaken. A harsh light was shining through the curtain-less windowpanes when she saw César crossing the hallway. Where, then, was he going, dressed in fine black clothes so early in the morning? 'You seem to forget that I'm getting married tomorrow,' he tossed out while walking past the foot of the ladder. She was clumsily wiping the windows with her big white hands. Tomorrow! Things could happen before tomorrow! The storm, for example, the sky was yellowish, the lake full of lightning, hail would be falling on their vineyards, their damned vineyards, they were the cause of all this evil with their distorted vinestocks, their terrifying bare dirt . . . César was coming back with Eugène—also in fine black clothes? —who tried to slip unnoticed into the bedroom from which the furniture had been removed.

'Eugène!' she shouted, still on her ladder. 'Where have you been?'

'Darling,' he said, trembling—she would in fact need a few minutes to come back down—'we've been at the town hall. The wedding has taken place.'

He fled onto the wooden balcony, locked the door, and remained there for hours, taking care not to soil his black clothes. She was coming heavily down off the ladder. 'Take these mattresses and these pieces of furniture back upstairs. This year, we won't be doing any cleaning.' Startled, the hired women went away to the kitchen and from there, their arms helplessly dangling, walked back through the village to their homes. The Adventist offered to consecrate the marriage on the lawn neatly raked by the servants of the rich patients, but the barefoot baroness, at the head of her cohort, might have walked through the throng, so they decided on the village church. César entered the church, trembling, expecting to see it sinking speechless, its arms raised, into the earth, like the children the evening before. Blanche was coughing softly and raising her hand to her veil. 'Oh,' the tailoress was thinking, grasping her chin and touching her face with two spread-out fingers, 'white is clearly not M'zelle Blanche's colour.' The evangelist began speaking, then stopped, his gaze focused on the wall, he raised his right hand, clicked his tongue like a stork, turned transparent, a glimmer of a smile lit up his face, everyone furtively turned his head; yet nothing happened, today was not the day. His hand fluttering around the pulpit came down heavily, he took up his speech again with a very strong voice, the dice, held aloft, came down. The newlyweds emerged holding on to each other and walked along the cemetery; over there next to the wall it seemed that the big flat rock that she had wanted for her grave was splitting. The schoolchildren were whispering, the lake suddenly appeared at the bend in the path, it was very dark out, it was one of those brief autumns, full of dead leaves, dead women, swirling winds, that last a few hours in midsummer.

'You'll see,' César said suddenly, 'we'll have a little boat, the *Danaé*.'

'But César, isn't *Danaé* the name of your brother's boat?

He stopped speaking. The carriage entered the forest. Raising his eyes, César was searching the sky. The air was so calm that the demolished tower was hanging down the side of the château like a swan's wing; a big yellowish cloud was rising on the horizon. But Blanche's relatives and cousins, who had come from the high plateaus where the vegetation consists either of one-inch flowers or web-footed plants as tall as black men, were jabbering away, fearless of the strange silence. Suddenly, as they were sitting at the table, the sound of cavalry was heard, everything became yellowish, the tablecloth, the glasses, the over-heated faces.

'Hail!'

César stood up, but he was held back.

'But it's hail. We can't just stay here.'

'You can't leave,' said Eugène. 'Stay, César. Do you think I wouldn't prefer being down there as well?'

He was clasping César's arm in a brotherly way.

'It's the edge of the downpour. Maybe Combe-vallière or Les Guerres won't be hit.'

'Hail,' Madame suddenly exclaimed. 'It's hailing. I knew this would happen, I'm always right.'

Until then, she had been staring like a savage at the guests without answering their questions, so much so that the head of the bride's good and decent aunt, sitting across from her, could be seen melting away like a wax bust exposed to heat. Then signs suddenly showed that Madame was going to laugh. Oh my God, the kitchen windowpanes that are going to shatter into pieces and wound the ruddy gleaming cook busying herself over her big lake trout so white and foam-coloured that César shuddered when he saw it lying on an English metal platter. But fortunately the windows were small and the embrasures deep enough to resist the lake storms, only one windowpane lacking putty fell out. Madame had imprisoned a lizard beneath her bunion-bumpy foot. 'Come near me, Marguerite,' she ordered. Marguerite was trembling with anger at not having been the first to get married. 'So come near me, how pretty Marguerite is, she's the flower, the beauty of the family. And so young . . . ,' she added, lowering her voice and nodding at the bride who was flinching under the weight of her veil. César, his arm was draped around the back of her chair, wouldn't be rowing the *Danaé* out for a half-hour on the sunset-lit waters over which empty winds chase after each other and either sow the waters with violets or dig a dark-blue river through the middle of the lake. Mélanie was stealing glances at César and bringing her hand to her tumultuous breasts. Madame had invited the gentleman farmer in vain. '*Shall we go?*' he asked while pushing his tawny moustache back up over his lip. 'All in all, my dear, we don't know them. They have a kind of château, but who was their mother?' Foolhardy fellow! Stung in the mouth eight days later by a wasp on a plum, he died. As to the painter who swam naked and swallowed raw snails, as to the young woman who came from Edom and who stopped whenever she saw a tower, both of whom were leaning on the fence separating them from the clinic, they joyfully shouted out greetings to the wedding party they were watching through the open door, the bent-over servant women, the black clothes already showing future scarecrows even as a spider bears the design of its web. A few inoffensive madmen wearing overalls and raking the gravel were sticking their flabby faces to the window.

'When's your wedding, Zoé?' sniggered Madame.

These were her last words. She thereafter pretended to sleep, sitting straight on a chair, her big hat, on which a feather boa was coiled, gently nodding up and down; from time to time she would barely lift her walled-up-woman's heavy hand, shooing away a fly from her broad face. After the storm, a breath of wind was blowing in from the lake and the pinewood sloping down all the way to the shore, one of the marvels of the world. It was surely not there where César could have found the children, the pinewood was rather far from Fraidaigue, a carriage was needed to go there, and when, God in heaven, would a carriage have been offered to those sensitive children! This time, it was a brake-carriage that would shuttle everyone between the clinic and the train station. César and Blanche were the first to take it, he stretched his neck to try to glimpse the damage caused by the hail, and he even made the coachman stop, then got out himself and went down into a vineyard, all the while running the risk of missing the train for Italy. In Milan, he bought a camera although he had very little money for the honeymoon. Where would they live when they returned? Later, later!

'No, don't take my picture, I'm too ugly, take a picture of the church,' she said softly.

Dressed in her grey travelling clothes, she was moving away from the Milanese church porch. Why shouldn't you wear grey, grey is your colour, blondes paint themselves up in grey! She moved still further away from the porch, gaily turned her back to César, leant on her red umbrella.

'No, I don't want to look at the camera, I'm too ugly, let me pretend to look at the church.'

She never asked, Where will we live? César raised the problem one evening in the restaurant, above a platter of seafood.

'As for us,' he said, balancing his fork on his index finger, ' I don't know very well . . . What are we going to do? Fraidaigue? The Maison d'En Haut? Demand my share? Perhaps go abroad?'

She shyly placed her hand on his.

'Whither thou goest, I will go; and where thou lodgest, I will lodge, thy God shall be my God . . . You know, César,' she added, blushing, 'I'm not the one who invented those words, they're in the Bible.'

She withdrew her hand and sipped a little Chianti . . . On the evening of the wedding, only Madame had kept her cool. Their wine! For what I care about it! Mélanie had drowned in alcohol her sorrow at seeing César leave on another woman's arm, they were all a little drunk when they ended up in an intimate family circle in the parlour of Fraidaigue, the three windows opening onto the night. The invisible lake was stirring its waves along the shore. They kept drinking while standing and talking noisily in the middle of the room; sitting on the velvet settee, Madame was hastily cleaning her fingernails and staring at them with disdain: Peasants! Drunkards!

'So your César's off to a start. We thought he'd never marry.'

'Oh, I myself really wanted this wedding to take place. César is our eldest child, our brother.' Eugène's eyes were brimming with tears. 'Is it a life, I ask you, to spend six months here . . . '

He hiccupped, excused himself politely, Adolphe brought him a spoonful of powered sugar.

'Here, Eugène. My little Eugène, take this!'

'It's to your credit to have convinced him to marry' —Eugène nodded his approval energetically—'for what are you going to do now?'

He shrugged his shoulders.

'He's our brother, our dear elder brother.'

Behind them they suddenly heard Madame's voice coming from the end of the parlour.

'Come, Eugène.'

'Come where, darling?'

She had stood up, her walled-up-woman's hands hanging straight down. The men fetched their hats.

'Come, Eugène. It's late.'

Unaware of the peril, only the pastor kept talking, his voice hissing between teeth worn down by preaching the Good Word: 'But what will you do when he comes back? If I may intercede, I'll do so willingly, very willingly.'

They were all hurrying towards the door, jostling one another to leave.

'We'll be thinking about his return, about the share, later,' she said slowly. 'Tonight I have other fish to fry. Where are you going, Eugène?'

'But they're leaving, darling, I need to accompany them.'

'They'll go down all by themselves.'

'But I need to close the doors.'

'Pooh! Leave everything open. Come, Eugène.'

From the stairway, they heard her loudly repeating on the threshold of their bedroom:

'Come, Eugène.'

The next day, she once again moved the trunks around in the garret, tufts of hair were breaking away from the big salt-and-pepper construction, a spider web remained attached to her green blouse decorated with guipures that hid her massive shoulders. Eugène stayed in bed. She climbed the tower staircase, began to groan. The sound could be heard all the way to the village. The houses thought that the ancient waves that had tilted them were coming back. The weather was strange all that summer: yellowish clouds, storms, the lake full of lightning. It's the baroness, they whispered, what's she going to do?

'We'll have to leave,' she said as soon as she had arrived at the stable. 'We're the ones who will live in this pigsty, yes, we, the Eugènes . . . '

'But you haven't reached that point,' reassured Édith with her soft, smothered voice, a needle threaded with black cotton stuck into her blouse.

'And what point have we reached, may I ask?'

She didn't wait for an answer. Off she went, driven out of everywhere, digging seeds out of her pocket, sowing them from her big trembling hands, and then suddenly uprooting vegetables from entire sections of the vegetable patch; good God, nothing must be left to them! And she was especially on the lookout for the children, who were merrily coming back home from school.

'Hey, hurry up,' she was shouting from afar. 'You'll just have time enough to pack up your things.'

The messenger was taking a breath of fresh air at her window across the way from the gate. 'You're scratching yourself, Isabelle,' she boldly whispered. 'Have you got lice? Be careful, if you let the lice come, they'll make a big braid with your hair and drag you into the lake.'

Frightened, Isabelle climbed the stairs, opened the door to her room, found her mother packing.

'Where's my doll?'

'I've just given it to Ol' Miss Gibaude, what would you do with it?'

César would have been delighted if he could have seen Isabelle and Abraham weeping in front of the empty cupboards while Madame was groaning at her window. But it seemed he was in Rome; no news from them, everything was going well. That afternoon, Blanche, leaning on the balustrade that encircled the excavations, holding her red umbrella, kept stubbornly turning her back on César. 'I'll wait,' he was saying, 'you'll end up turning back around.' She was laughing: 'No! No! I'm too ugly, take pictures of the Capitoline Hill geese instead.' My friend, my wife! How she laughs! She didn't laugh like that before, with the Adventists ... Her skinny, hunched body, that whirling umbrella! Ah, this time the children have vanished, good for them; I'll no longer be in danger of meeting up with Zoé in the antechamber of the old kitchen on the second floor, her mourning apron hanging down longer than her dress . . . Behind their back, the Jubilee crowd was shouting and probably hurrying towards the pope being fanned with ostrich feathers. 'I'm too ugly,' she kept chuckling. How these Italian crowds shout. At Fraidaigue, Madame, who was groaning at the window, spotted a buggy coming down from the train station.

'Ah, it's the Aldophes!' she said in a languishing voice, using both hands to push up the big construction on her head. 'Do you hear me, Eugène, the Adolphes are arriving.'

It was stifling hot. They attached the horse alongside the gate, Mélanie stumbled over an invisible animal and her hip struck the back of a garden bench.

'So here you are, at last,' said Semiramis, sitting on the velvet settee and awaiting them. 'Calm down, Adolphe, you're making my head spin with your pacing up and down, and you, Eugène, go fetch a bottle of wine. We might as well empty the wine cellar, don't you think? . . . So say something. What are we going to do?'

'But . . . what's the matter?' asked Adolphe, holding his lorgnon in the air after wiping it on the tip of his waistcoat. 'We've just dropped by to see you, that's all. And to see the vineyards. It's a disaster, from what we've heard.'

'Oh, a disaster . . . One mustn't exaggerate. Combevallière, where lots of hail fell, was going to be replanted next year, anyway, and . . . '

'Shut up, Eugène. You and your eternal vineyards! I'm not teaching you anything new by reporting that your brother César, who's the eldest child after all, has got married. He's now on his honeymoon in Italy. Honeymoon, pooh!'

'So what.'

'So what? . . . But don't you understand? They're going to come back, and where will we live? In the woodpile?'

'But here, of course . . . It's so big. There'll be enough room for two households, won't there?'

'Where? Where?' she shouted, suffocating with rage. 'Where's the room for two households in this place? Oh, my father told me so.'

When he was walking on the pavement along the fiacre. It was becoming clearer that he wasn't as old as that, after all.

She kept repeating while spraying them with saliva: 'Do you think there's room enough for two households in this place? We have children! And live on what? We'll barely get by, this year, we'll have to take out a mortgage. Oh no, I know, we'll have to give in. It's his turn to live in the château. He's going to throw us out on the roads.'

'Let's not judge,' said Adolphe softly, adjusting his lorgnon and looking around.

'Either throw us out, or you out,' she continued.

'How's that? . . . ' he suddenly cried. 'Us? But we're not concerned by this. We already have Zoé.'

'And why wouldn't he go and live in the Maison d'En Haut, if I may ask? It's up to you to make the stable habitable or leave for America.'

'What? What?' he repeated, staggered. 'Come on, he only wants to live here, in the château.'

'Oh, leave me alone with your château. And now that I think of it, he's always told me that he didn't want to own Fraidaigue because of the tower that reminded him of something. No, no, it's the Maison d'En Haut that he'll claim.'

'And you're standing here without doing anything?' squealed Adolphe. 'Let's do something, for God's sake!'

'Adolphe!' moaned Mélanie.

'Ah!' she murmured, now ignoring them, wringing her walled-up-woman's hands. 'Why did I prevent him from marrying that Gwen, who was rich, an only child? . . . You, you stop drinking.'

Eugène had set the bottle on the piano, between the painting of a girl classmate standing at an ivy-framed window and the photo of Madame's so-called parents. He quietly walked over to the bottle on his rubbery feet and poured himself a glass without making any noise.

'It's also your fault. Môssieu chats with the fishermen, the wine-growers heap praise on him because he gives them two litres instead of one, without giving a thought to his own children, soon to be ruined by all these bad years. That young man would spend his time in the stable. What was he thinking about, if I may ask?'

Whether he has married this girl or that one, he now lives with her, kisses her, they sleep together in that Italy that I'll never see. Or only with Adolphe.

'Let's wait and see,' ventured Eugène, standing near the piano. 'The last word hasn't been pronounced.'

'Oh,' sighed Madame, 'of course, all sorts of things could happen, a train accident, bandits, malaria. But try to count on Providence!'

She shrugged her massive shoulders, hastily cleaned her fingernails, then suddenly, throwing her head back, began to groan. Ah, I'd forgotten! Ah, he's going to come back, throw me out of the house! She stood up and stormed out like a madwoman; regretfully abandoning his half-filled glass, Eugène dashed after her. Adolphe was pacing up and down, distractedly pouring himself some wine, intently staring at Madame's parents without seeing them. The other two weren't coming back, so Adolphe and Mélanie ended up returning to the Maison d'En Haut. The villagers on the lookout spotted them riding ever father away on their buggy, shoulder to shoulder.

'That César,' she muttered, 'what a wretch!'

'Let's not judge,' she said.

'To the cellar!' shouted Semiramis. 'But I hadn't thought of that! I'm going to open the casks!'—I need to follow her, prevent her at all costs from turning the spigots—'Over there, that vase, the big one, the twelve-thousand-litre one!'—But doesn't she even know that it has been empty for years?—'But it's empty, nothing's flowing, ah, what jackasses! So let's open this one and that one too, for God's sake'—I'll come back down tonight when she's asleep and close them. 'So drink, Eugène, don't hesitate, here's a glass! Swallow!' She never drinks wine, despises it, has always despised it. 'So drink, Eugène, drink!' Good God, she's going to get drunk, I'll have to carry her back upstairs! 'Two thousand, six thousand, nine thousand five! The wine-press room full of their wretched wine! An entire wine-growing year going to hell!'—Good God! she's still drinking, one glass, two glasses, her hand's shaking, she's pouring half of it off to the side, what a pity; but it looks like she's now opened all the casks and is getting ready to leave.

'You see, Eugène,' she stated, applying herself, 'I lock the cellar door, put the key in this hole in the wall, where no one will think of touching it, are you listening, Eugène? I'm putting put the key . . . '

He grasped her by the waist in the stairway; how enormous she was, and so heavy, a world! She was rearranging her chignon: 'I've hidden the key in the hole in the wall, take in this wine smell, it's the first time I like it. But why should I go to bed when it's broad daylight? I've never been lazy.'

She stretched out on her catafalque-bed, leaning her stone shoes against Eugène's stomach; he hugged her legs in his arms and cranked them in circles like a winepress. The next morning she didn't get up, why should she? She was groaning, her head turned to the wall. Isabelle, Abraham and Ulysse were huddled in the room where the summer toys are kept. That afternoon, the messenger saw them going sadly down the lane; sitting on the threshold of her house, Ol' Miss Gibaude was rocking Isabelle's doll. 'You're scratching yourself, Isabelle,' the old ladies were whispering. 'Be careful, the lice are going to make a braid with your hair and drag you down to the lake.' A yellow leaf was whirling in the calm air, the farmer's children were playing with Ulysse's little stove against the garden wall. A loud voice could be heard wailing upstairs, it got closer.

'So she seems to be on her feet?'

'She's calling out for you.'

'Isabelle! My poor little Isabelle!'

The girl lowered her head.

'Isabelle! Where are you? Oh, You no longer have an aunt! Your pretty Aunt Blanche you loved so! Where is she? In heaven, my child.'

What's the matter with her, the frightened villagers were wondering. She has received a telegram, the calamity has happened to M'zelle Blanche. My God, her poor parents! And that poor baroness! Listen to how she's screaming and wailing. 'Oh, oh, Blanche! I who loved her so much!'

'Darling, you're going to make yourself sick. Drink a little tea.'

The boiling hot tea gave her the hiccups, she pushed the cup away and began groaning again.

'Abraham, my poor little Abraham, hic, you don't have an, hic, aunt any more, your pretty Aunt, hic, Blanche whom you loved so much, hic, whom we all loved.'

Blanche dead! Brooding, Eugène was biting his thumbnail.

'Oh, say whatever you wish, hic, I had an inkling. When I saw her leave, hic . . . '

The farmer's children had just finished the roast placed on a small board between two stones, Louis was washing the two little metal plates, it was the first day of the harvesting holiday.

'Where are you going, darling?'

Madame was going down the stairs, enveloped in her black silk coat, gripping her gold-knobbed umbrella in her strong hand and wearing her Mary Stuart–like hat.

'But darling, where do you wish to go? You've just experienced a terrible emotional shock.'

So he hadn't read it? The telegram? 'Inform parents.'

'And you're going there?'

Shall we go?, the winged horse behind Blanche's neck had said. When the screams became so loud that César turned around, a bright red tramway was looming over him like a mountain, he jumped to the side, a cracking sound was heard, the beast's nose braked to a stop in Blanche's back, shoved her against the balustrade that partly gave way and hung over the abyss with the mutilated body sticking to the railings.

'Don't go there,' pleaded Eugène, they probably already know.

'Don't be an imbecile. How else will they know?' she shouted, gathering up her dress and dashing out. 'Leave me alone, time is running out.'

She hurried as fast as she could, but it was hot, her mourning clothes were cumbersome, and she lost precious minutes taking back Ulysse's little stove from the farmer's children and perching it out of reach on the roof girder of the gazebo. One of the two metal plates rolled towards the back of the courtyard, this is all that remained of their short happiness; and it was the first day of the harvesting holiday! (For the doll, Madame couldn't get it back so easily, Ol' Guibaude defended herself, Madame came back brooding, with a bloody cheek.) Alas, she arrived at the clinic too late, her face covered with sweat, her unwieldy umbrella swinging from her wrist, and she couldn't even see them since they had shut themselves up inside their room. Hopefully, that afternoon, they had joyfully observed the blue-and-gold lake, the avenue of beech trees yellowed by the autumn. Nevermore! Blanche! Blanche! César brought her back home, dead. Was it possible? Just when she had become his friend, his companion, the only human being... He was looking through the train door at the countryside flying past in the night and at the telegraph wires constantly stopped in their flight. It's not known where swifts sleep, they leave the earth towards two o'clock in the morning, go off to sleep together somewhere above the clouds . . . My God! Blanche! It's not known where swifts sleep, they go off to sleep together somewhere above the clouds . . . It's not known . . . The aged evangelist was at the train station, leaning on his wife. As well as Madame, who was holding down her Mary Stuart–like hat with its large crepe veil.

'To Fraidaigue,' ordered César. 'It's closer,' he added, blushing.

The porters started out, a few button roses picked in passing were hastily tossed on the black cloth. The coffin was placed between two velvet-upholstered chairs, César was gazing at the lake, at the gulls whose piercing squeals were announcing autumn.

'César,' said Madame, entering and giving off a draft of cold air, 'César, do believe that . . . '

He turned around, no, he wasn't wrong, she could not keep herself from smiling slightly, one of her deep-sea-diver teeth could be spotted, it could be spotted every day during all those days, even during the funeral service when she clasped her walled-up-woman's big, lividly white fingers beneath her black veil. She sat down on the settee, distractedly cleaning her fingernails while César remained standing, motion-less, in front of the coffin.

'Do believe, César, that if we could do it all over again . . . No, really, I sense that I'm no longer attached to this château.'

She sprayed out a little saliva.

'It's here, César, where you would have lived with . . .'

She extended her chin towards the black cloth.

'Me? What do I care about the château?! I don't care about anything any more. Ah, how I envy her, dead so young. Because that's what she was: young. Young and pretty. Yes, really, for me she was pretty, with her foamy blond hair, she looked like her father, especially from the side. To say that a month ago she was here, looking out this window, with me speaking to her. Me.

'Was she really disfigured? And if . . . Similar cases have been seen. She might have received only a shock.

'Wouldn't it be better . . .'

She once again pointed her chin towards the coffin. César turned back and went towards the settee.

'No, César, let's say I didn't say anything, no, no, César, but you're crazy, you're going to strangle me, you're joking, César.'

He let go of her, once again, let his own heavy hands fall to his sides, his walled-up-man's hands, and paid no attention, as he stood in front of the coffin, to whether she was leaving the parlour or, sitting back down, beginning to hastily clean her fingernails once again. If he didn't decide to drown Madame the next day by inviting her to go fishing after having removed a board from the bottom of the *Danaé*—if he himself drowned, who would find the children on the beach? and they had come back, like a burden, after the death of poor Blanche, a big swan chasing them, clacking its spatulate orange beak—if he hadn't managed to stick Madame on a spit, to strangle her, to drown her, then Abraham neither would have fallen from the cornice and come back to life just as soon, nor have embarked on a lifeboat during the storm and returned safe and sound, and little Ulysse still remained, the youngest child, with his green candle and the freckles on his pale, square face. A terrible winter was approaching, following upon that bad year of rain and hail that sticks in wine-growers' memories; some vineyards were not even harvested. Few grapes, few walnuts. The walnut trees had leaves only, like that year when the inheritor of the Maison d'En Haut, the former little ogre, dropped like lightning through the branches. A cistern stands below the tree, an iron-covered stone cube convenient for cracking pilfered walnuts, and his head burst open on it. The Maison d'En Haut thereby came down by heritage to his former victims, his children. At Fraidaigue, draught excluders had to be placed against the windows, Eugène himself made them in the garden. It snowed as early as October, no one dared to tell César to leave. The fur-enveloped stranger was heading for the train station to the silent trot of a horse pulling a swan-necked sleigh, and he was surprised that he could no longer hear the dull thudding of the lake against the shore. This was because the lake had frozen over. The rising waves were motionless, and the village children, gleefully shouting as they walked on the curved-down crests, spotted the Savoyards coming out of their abodes and, as they moved forward, their faces increasingly lost their sky-blue colour. Even the duchess of Tourronde left her big château.

'Eugène! Can you hear me? Now where's your brother again? I happen to know: he's on the lake with the Savoyards.'

On the lake, feet instead of wind are staking out paths and Rim's old rowboat, caught unawares by the freeze, eternally dips its bow into the water. Amélie the laundress is going down to feed the imprisoned gulls, the ladies of the sewing circle are bringing them jugs of warm tea, the entire village is walking on the water. So they were still alive, those old men with their red eyes and pale complexions? '*It's great fun*,' the gentleman farmer deigns to remark to the regent who replies that the lake is well patronized today and who, in hear heart, renounces her washwoman-mother. A gulfstream flowing behind the crests of the waves cuts out a square of black water. Moreover, here's solemn Ulysse with his green candle and two small purplish hands, his two other, woollen, hands are attached to a string.

'Uncle César!'

César grabbed him by the neck, that chicken-neck children have; he bent it down towards the breach, a big, tall wave of ice was separating them from the crowd, but Ulysse was gripping the edge like a cat.

'Uncle César!'

His voice was fading away across the expanse. Suddenly Uncle César told him not to scream, that he had only wanted to frighten him. Perched atop the wave, the messenger was watching them and laughing; she was wearing that green rep dress that no one, except César, seemed to recognize. Hey, let her take my curtain! May nothing come between me and the lake any more except the fishnets drying on the beach. And may Ulysse, who has fled, run off all pale between the waves of ice. With her hen-beaked nose, her head bald like an old judge's, the messenger, who's been the same for years, ever since the fatal night when she carted off the dead child's layette, nearly got a leg trapped in the ice like the gulls. The foehn began to blow, the village retreated to the shore, a few Savoyard women drowned. The next day it was snowing, the heavy snow-birds falling silently from the branches. Ulysse came home from school, grabbed his hoop stick which was lying on the hallway sideboard, let it drop like a tit-mouse letting a tiny leaf drop, and he couldn't pick it up because it was now a thousand miles away. He managed to struggle up to his room, nestle into his bed, his thick dirty little hands clutching the cover under his chin. He and Abraham would wash in an enamel basin and empty it out the window. After an hour, when his hair started falling over his eyes, he couldn't push it back with an impatient hand. He was taken to the infirmary. Coming back from delivering five thousand litres of wine to the Jurassian merchant, César ran into the procession as he turned into the street with the houses tilted because of ancient waves. A dog running diagonally to the infirmary rushed inside the courtyard then rushed out so fast that no one knew if it was indeed, or not, Faraud, the black and fire-coloured setter that would place its square head on Ulysse's knees scratched by the cedar branches at that spot where they had spent the summer building a tree house. Never again would Ulysse climb into the cedar, he still could row, but César, full of love and concern, would need to pick him up tenderly and set him inside the boat. Madame massaged him for two weeks.

'I'll myself massage him every morning,' said Eugène.

'Yes, yes, Eugène.'

He would just be able enough to count grape-picker's baskets or gather poppy seed. For weeks, for months in the past, the children would watch the pink poppies blossoming at face level. There was no doubt that César was now slowly getting closer to the children. He had only Eugène's wedding, announced by that damned fiacre, to get through, only ten comings and goings, at each equinox, between Fraidaigue and the Maison d'En Haut where he filled the stable with his shouting and his pitchfork jabs. Émile, the ward of the commune, spends his time pushed up against the wall, an arm over his face, managing to escape only by slipping between the horse's legs; having taken refuge in his damp room infested with earwigs, he uses his wretched purplish hand to stir a black liquid in a chipped jam jar. At about the same time as the scarecrow garment, that moth-eaten wedding garment, recovers its place in the closet at Fraidaigue, as its buttons like the hard backs of beetles get covered with cloth once again and emerge new from the earth, appeared the damned fiacre that had so often jolted along in their memories. The two brothers who were spending a few days, it is no longer known why, in this city of clockmakers, saw it going by, the horse being walked, the big wheels squeaking on the snow. Right next to it, holding a white leather glove reaching out from inside the fiacre, was a solemn man walking on the pavement. César smelled of lily-of-the-valley, he had placed a top hat on his thick red hair. The trees along the avenue seemed immense, a lit-up citadel glimpsed through the fog announced the ballroom in the distance.

> *When everything is over*, Eugène was singing softly,
> *When our-our-our beautiful dream is dying,*
> *Who's there in that fiacre,*
> *giving her hand to her father?*
> *It's a lovely young lady—*
> *Ha ha ha, our-our-our beautiful dream . . .*

and they tightened their undertaker's ties. They saw coming out of the halted fiacre a woman whose gown was so vast that her father, accompanying her to the ball, had walked on the pavement and gave her his hand in order not to be left behind. The bust that climbed the staircase in front of them plunged into the white corolla. Other busts, lined up on chairs along the wall, were being fanned silently by solid arms almost entirely hidden by long white gloves. The black garments showing the future scarecrow set up in the vineyards, its top hat, its arms stretched out as if cruci-fied, were crowding against the doors of the ballroom.

'That young woman over there, isn't she the one from the fiacre?'

The young woman from the fiacre. A low bulging forehead, big grey eyes. César, smelling of lily-of-the-valley, and Eugène, with his bright-pink complexion, seemed unconcerned when they left the spot where they were waiting and moved across the wooden floor, their reddish, still-childlike hands dangling out from the end of their black sleeves.

'César! My child! What are you doing here? I haven't seen you for centuries.'

The old godfather! Twenty-two years earlier, his wan head, big and light like eggshell, was bending over a newborn baby. The newborn baby was looking with disgust at the ceiling and thrusting out his red-dish fists lighter than air.

'Godfather . . . Yes . . . You see . . .'

Eugène was walking away, crossing expanses of the wooden floor, bowing to the young woman and inviting her to dance . . . Her big eyes were reflecting the light from the gas lamps, she was tall and strong. Then she ate a biscuit without taking off her white leather gloves. César had come across his godfather fallen from the moon, his big head light like eggshell.

213

The gas was being turned down, the asbestos handle was blackening at the edges, the young woman left on her father's arm, breaths formed rifle cartridges that were shooting out of lips in the thick fog. Eugène never understood what notion came to him, the next morning, to marry the young woman at the ball. Probably because of that fiacre which had been swaying between its two big wheels squeaking on the snow and from which a gloved hand reached out; inside the fiacre, a big corolla could be imagined, and at the heart of the corolla legs sheathed in thick silk knee socks. 'And what if I proposed to that young woman?' he wondered as he awoke, raising the lid of the cream-coloured chamber pot decorated with pink roses. And what, César, still in bed, was wondering, if he were going to meet the godfather? The fog was clearing, the clockmakers, their magnifying glasses forgotten on their forehead, it was Sunday, were leaning out of the windows, the young woman, wearing a cream-coloured gingham dress, cotton gloves on her strong hands, was getting ready to water the aspidistra which, in vain, was trying to escape out of a window that was narrow because of the harsh winters. Eugène explained that he owned a château at the edge of the lake. And all this while suddenly wondering: But what am I doing here? He started speaking about the godfather. What? Monsieur Anselme? they exclaimed. He nodded, rather satisfied. The marriage was quickly arranged because of the château and especially because of Monsieur Anselme. Everything was so simple, famine, plague or war would of course no longer exist, and the most recent harvests had brought one hundred thousand litres under the winepress. At thirty centimes per litre, and only two thousand francs of expenditures, one could be excused for getting married in twenty-four hours. Simply, the father showed until his death, which in fact quickly occurred, an embarrassment that Eugène could not immediately explain; during his death throes, his dying man's heavy hand was waving in front of his face in an attempt to chase away, shatter, destroy an infrangible stare. Back at Fraidaigue, César beat the little servant in the stable for the first time. Then he wandered about the snow-covered terrace; the snow barely stays in this area, no longer than a wedding day takes.

'And you, my César,' says the godfather, whose head tilts to the left, to the right, like an enormous empty egg, 'when's your turn?'

'Oh, César has the makings of a bachelor!'

But the godfather persists.

'You're of course going to move in here, into Fraidaigue, but he could take the Maison d'En Haut, couldn't he?'

'What about me?' says Adolphe, the youngest brother.

'Oh, me?' mutters César, 'I'll never get married.'

'That's the right thing to do,' the groom suddenly cries in a hoarse voice.

'You're right about that,' adds the godfather. 'Women . . . '

He winks with an eye which has no eyelashes. My God, shut the doors! Shut them! A draught nearly blew away his enormous light head because of the foolhardy bride and groom leaving for their wedding night. The next morning, César, leaning his elbows on a windowsill, was gazing at the two equal-sized meadows of the roof and the gulf where the boats from Meillerie slowly land, their sails down. Seen from above, Eugène, who was walking along the beach, his hands behind his back, seemed all huddled up. A half-hour later Madame climbed into the train carriage, the steps sagging under her weight, the wine-growers saw her going by, sitting straight on her rubber mat; in her family, a rubber mat was always stuffed into the suitcases of young newlyweds leaving on their honeymoon.

'I noticed her at the ball,' said Eugène, dressed in black and with a bright-pink complexion, to the school chum whom he met in the hallway. 'I proposed to her the next day, saying to myself: Why not? The year had been good, one hundred thousand litres sold at thirty centimes, what do you think? Her father immediately agreed . . . Unfortunately . . . ,' he added after a while, but no one knew if he had said this softly or simply thought it. At dawn, they took a gondola at the bottom of the staircase across from the pink palace, he bought her a coral necklace on St Mark's Square, the mixed voices of the strolling crowd resembled the din before a show begins. I saw her at her first ball; her bulging forehead, her long brown braids, her big grey eyes reflecting the light from the gas lamps, her arms filling out so exactly the white leather of her long gloves. Alas! He was twenty years old, the fiacre was moving along the pavement covered with brown sugar, a father was holding a mysterious hand. 'I proposed, and they immediately agreed.' Pensive, wearing a chequered carrick cape, she was leaning on a cardboard boulder and gazing at the billows, her young husband behind her was rocking back and forth on his heels and tip-toes and stretching his neck to see the sea. At this very moment, the embassy attaché, still unaware of Madame's existence, was visiting his tenant farmers, and in the big kitchen draped with hanging ears of maize the farmwife was feeding her bambino, his face black with flies.

Shall we go? the horse behind César's neck was whispering. He was being beckoned to, he suddenly heard a shrill sound of trumpets: the children! He rushed off, but what he picked up in the street, between the tilted houses, was a pumpkin stem. Damn! He'd arrive on time one day when a green trumpet would by lying there, when he would find the children, luminous, indestructible; for the future had slowly closed in front of him ever since Eugène's marriage with the young woman of the fiacre. Now that he was married, Eugène would take Fraidigue. But what about the lands and the Maison d'En Haut, rented out ever since the ogres' deaths? It would go to Adolphe. That would be his share. But César? Oh, César has the stuff of a bachelor. The nomad, the D.P., was then taking refuge at the farm, listening to the liquid manure dripping outside of the dark fire smouldering at the heart of the properties. Like a hanged man—so often crucified or hanged by Madame, who would stand back a little, contemplating her work, bending her globe-sized head to her shoulder—he was losing interest in the present and the future, he was looking at his red hair in the black liquid manure, his red hair tenderly pressed against the grey-feathered skirt. Burdened with those thousands of images that others destroy just as soon in order to keep, like merchants, only whatever might be useful, he staggered out of the stable, mixing up east and west, time and space.

'He drinks. Oh, that man drinks. He's my cross.'

Whatever he did, none of his acts seemed to modify the material world. The unfortunate events, Well-Well's arrival from the train station, Gwen's departure with Fritz, meeting up with the godfather at the doors of the ball, Blanche's death—all in all, he had merely waited for them to happen. Who could now prevent the nomad, the disinherited brother, from committing himself, without going so far as to get married, like Eugène, to the hazy country of the children, from leaving behind this fragment of time even as one leaves behind a fragment of space, from dropping straight down instead of continuing to progress horizontally? Naturally, this was his perfectly personal system, a private conversation between himself and the world.

'Hey, look at him leaving the stable! He's staggering. All Isabelle's suitors . . . '

Little mattered Madame's words, spawned in her big, empty head: he was the one who was right; for one can count from one hundred to one as easily as one can from one to one hundred, and doesn't the lake, during the hot August days, sometimes slant down to the mouth of the Rhone by inverting its slight slope? One could thus begin with Isabelle's most recent suitor, the man from the canton of Uri—a gold earring dangling from his left ear—move along the events, strolling on the margins of life like a child whom adults, speaking about time, schedules and woollen long johns, imperceptibly push off to those fringes of land inseparable from the waters. Lumbering forward in her bunion-embossed shoes, Madame was chatting about hygiene, architecture and logarithms, attracting Isabelle's suitors and looking them over closely, most of them would flee into the virgin forest, sometimes she deigned to take a walk in the blue gardens hanging in front of the windows. Mélanie's marriage was announced, preceded by a herd of half-wild horses, Zoé was warming her fingers with their excessively long nails against the emerald-green stove, Eugène and Madame were going off to Italy, Madame was sitting on a rubber mat in accordance with her poor mother's instructions. With this last obstacle—Eugène's marriage—removed, César was doubtless going to find the children. For they weren't dead, one would have known so otherwise. He wasn't searching for them around the Maison d'En Haut, on the avenue that the little ogre's brake-carriage would go down, its four wheels squeaking cheerfully and, as if during a morning of festivities, waving its red-and-white-striped curtains and slatted sides while the children watched them leave; Zoé was holding her doll's arm, her mourning apron longer than her dress, her black cotton stockings crumpled over her iron-tipped shoes, the visitors from the Franche-Comté were pinching their ears until blood came.

'Hey, look at these rude little kids. Come on, come on, Mathilde, we're going to miss the brake-carriage.'

Sometimes the great ogre rolled up his sleeves, cut the children to bits, put them in the salting tub at the foot of the staircase of the old kitchen. He perched Eugène on a hay wagon, the servile servants were laughing while holding out pitchforkfuls to him, a pink sainfoin flower had been his only friend ever since the turtledove's death, with the hay that murmured beautiful incomprehensible things, with the setter that placed its pug-nosed muzzle on its paws and sighed, 'Poor Little One!' Eugène's mourning apron made the visiting lady, who laughing only two days after his mother's death, feel ashamed while struggling to fasten her pink suspender on her enormous thigh. In the evening, while the ogres were resting on the terrace, the children circled the house, blowing into their trumpets, seeking the right sound, similar, hostile— according to Tom Tit, *Amusing Science*—that would make the house shatter like crystal. They were walking further into the countryside, holding hands, drunk like little bumblebees, they would see, leaning their heads on their shoulders, great majestic faces at the corner of a roof, between the roots of trees. Surely they could only have fled the Maison d'En Haut, having had to haunt the beaches, the unfinished grounds, the houses keeping the memory of ancient waves. And after all, if he didn't find the children, nothing, thought César, would keep him from going back into this strange haze, and this time, by Jove, to invite Madame to go fishing.

'How's that, César, you're inviting me to come with you? Don't you think the weather? . . . '

And delighted, she embarks, her lorgnon pinned to her harsh bosom, holding her Mary Stuart–like hat down flat. That hat was the first to fly off in the storm; after the hat, her bra, since she was bobbing just below the surface, sometimes on her back and sometimes on her stomach, then one of her big fat fingers of which she was so proud, then her corset that the children found washed up on the undulating sand between a rusty spring and one of the gentleman farmer's yellow shoes. From the top of the glassworks tower, bedecked with flowerlike porcelain insulators, the director was watching César drowning Madame and rowing pensively back to the shore; like a flight of birds, the water was dividing into a triangle beneath the bow. He might also have killed Madame by shooting her with his regulation military rifle; he had sometimes amused himself by placing on the stable window the alder stick whose bark he had patiently cut into spirals. Bella would jolt back in a big noise of hooves and floor-boards, Madame would be walking down the allée, followed by Eugène carrying pelargoniums in a moist newspaper from which some of the compost was falling out. 'Idiot,' she would mutter while squashing some spittle with her bunion-embossed shoe. But what's César up to? Upon my word, doesn't he seem to be aiming at us with his military rifle? At me? At his brother? At his little Ugène? He took shelter below the gazebo—bang, bang—Madame dropped dead. César laughed all by himself but then became serious at the thought, wasn't he running the risk, in this area covered with an ever-thicker mist, where he kept stumbling over vestiges, fragments and abandoned efforts, of meeting up with the appalling little ogre near the children? Strangely, his darkened memory struggled to remind him that the little ogre had fallen from the walnut tree, that his head had shattered on the stone cistern, and that, after his cremation, only a handful of ashes remained, that his mother had closed them up in a tiny satin bag and placed them inside her reticule. As to the children, they were living, honoured like orphans. At the place of honour during their parties. Their processions. Even on this earth with its tinny light to which he would return *whenever he wished*, the

camera lens was already focusing on troops of children, groups, hordes, under the bridges of Rome, on
the squares of the USSR, along lakes and seas, children
tightly packed together, compressed between two
wars, and the busy stupid swans were forcing their way
through their threatening throng and turning over a
fish with their spatulate orange beaks. But the adults
would put their hands over their eyes and ears so as not
to see and hear them, they would move house constantly so as not to be born, to live and to die in the
same house where they would run the risk, in the
evening, of meeting up with the children coming down
the wooden staircase barely lit by the tiny window of
the old kitchen. Meanwhile, the haze was thickening
enough to be cut with a knife, the brave nomad tried
to follow his footsteps back, but time, stretching like
a rubber band, was cruelly striking him in the face,
blood was flowing down over his clothes, over that
frightening grey greatcoat. May anyone wishing to
leave stable ground be warned! All the same, this was
indeed the country of the children, the sky had been set
flat down on a rectangular world, they could touch it
by raising their hands, gaze at the motionless sun in
space through bits of glass, make use of the sunlight to
write their names on little notebooks with oil-cloth
covers, a pink poppy was blooming all year long at face
level, no more springs and autumns than in the centre

of the earth—the centre of the earth?—summer merely a bar of blue sky between two half-closed shutters, Adolphe sitting on his little chamber pot suddenly flew off through this luminous breach by beating his short wings; César glimpsed him standing on the cornice. Adolphe! Adolphe! No reply. But two walls at his side could be seen getting bigger, and, between them, César was searching for the invisible stars of the day; by Jove, could the children indeed be at once present and invisible like stars? He thought once again of the April sky speckled with blue windows, the tilted angels in *trompe l'oeil*, then the haze darkened even more, all sailing was suspended, the sails were rising like high white flat triangular towers. He tried to cut through this haze with his military knife, he had broken the bottle opener that day when they were eating bread rolls and sardines on a bench of the Pincian Hill in order to save money. But what he was still taking for haze, so thick it would have to be cut through with a knife, was the earth, by Jove! He tried to pull out his pocket watch, his fob already full of dirt, his father had won this turnip at the 1887 Federal Shooting Match and had often told him how a storm was threatening, the sun pouring its tinny rays on the square where the festivities were taking place, on Numa Droz sporting a top hat and shouting from his platform, lifting towards the sky his blood-red forearms, the prize-watches violently clinking against an immense red-velvet wall, the dead popping up like matches into the air with every shot. Earth! Earth! He thought once again with sympathy of Jules to whom he had said without shuddering, 'Oh, you, you'll drink till the end of time,' forgetting the second horse of the hitched-up team, the end of all spaces; it was an October evening, the monumental doors closed after the wine had been brought in, a suspended hare was bleeding from its mouth into the courtyard of the inn. Did he regret his escape? Does one regret sinking headfirst into Semiramis' black gardens? Does the fox regret the air and the sky? Don't believe, however, that there are no more seasons for this nomad who has at last found his home. In the past, his departures and returns would take place at the equinoxes. But now: 'By Jove,' he said, his mouth crammed with earth, 'we must be in April, here's the eranthis hyemalis starting to come back down; in July, the early rose potato is almost ripe.' Except for Adolphe, whom he had glimpsed for a moment on the cornice, it's true that he hadn't been able to spot the children in this haze. But he felt only perfect indifference, a deep joy while slowly swimming as the months went by between each movement, and indeed blood was no longer flowing down over this very handy grey greatcoat. Sometimes a little moisture indicated to him that he was going beneath the lake, sometimes coming back towards Fraidaigue where he would meet up with white violets, a mole, briar roots, greenish coins, immense pink ants, and vinestocks ploughing like ploughshares the earth of the vineyards run through by air and lightning.